CRIMEWAVE N

TRANSGRESSIO

ISSN 1463 1350 ⁂ ISBN 978-0-9553683-0-1 ⁂ © 2007 Crimewave on behalf of all contributors ⁂ Published in the UK by TTA Press, 5 Martins Lane, Witcham, Ely, Cambs CB6 2LB ⁂ Further information, discussion forum, online subscriptions and back issues on www.ttapress.com, and in the conributors section of this issue ⁂ Subscribe now to four issues for just £22 UK • £26 EUROPE • £30 ROW, by cheque payable to TTA Press or credit card and sent to the above address or online at the website ⁂ Thanks to Peter Tennant for proofreading and editorial assistance ⁂ Edited by Andy Cox ⁂ Set in Warnock Pro ⁂ Printed in the UK by Cambridge University Press

BLUE MORPHO

SHELLEY COSTA

Mo McCallum didn't hold it against the lake that it was so deep it took two divers to bring up her daughter's body on the day of the regatta. Amy's little foot – she was just eighteen months old – was caught on a stick that had actually threaded itself through the slats in one of her clear jelly shoes, the divers pointed out. The other shoe was nowhere to be found. And so a stick coated in soft algae, in the deep, black part of this Canadian lake was all that stood between Mo McCallum and her little girl. Depending on how you looked at it, one of the neighbors tried telling her, that stick was what kept Amy from drifting away from them all.

How Mo McCallum looked at it was this: her child was dead.

There was no father to share her grief – she was raising Amy alone – and no parents of her own, anymore, to wrap her up until she could forget the sight of those divers, whenever that might be. It was late afternoon by the time they found Amy two hundred feet off the southeast point of the Wellers' island. By then, power boats from elsewhere on the lake had come in, rumbling in a watchful circle, like some strange factory ready to process the child back to life.

Steve Beck stood offshore in waist-high water the whole time, shouting to the divers, hurling curses into the air, and Mo stood shaking on the rocks in the heat, wondering who he was, the crazy man screaming in the shallows, when she had just yesterday been making wedding plans with him. He had sailed the race in his Invitation, which was all he could afford on this lake where dinghies were just so many playthings, and he had lost the race becalmed off the southeast point of the island, on the far side of the final marker.

Rick Wakeman had rowed out to the divers, who were lifting the body, all the colors of her gone, all the yellow of her hair, her romper, gone, only lake water streaming off her everywhere. Steve was swimming out to the boat then, his cries bursting every time he took a breath, and Mo despised him forever, watching love, too, stream back into the lake off her little girl's body, disappearing into silver ripples as they lifted her into the boat to Rick. Steve, who had suddenly decided to race, too, when he had told her he was watching Amy. Where was he? Where was she? Where in God's name were any of them?

She rounded on the other cottagers. "Didn't you see her? Didn't any of you see her? You were all right here." Mo started shrieking, ripping her nails down her own face, wanting only to take out her eyes, that had somehow failed. She was off her feet, then, her back arched, lifted into others' arms, crying to the sky that looked very far away. *"Didn't any of you see her?"*

And although heads were shaking – some, because they had to answer, and some, because the world was unbearable – no one said a thing. But in the early afternoon of the annual regatta in 2000, when Amy McCallum walked into the lake in her yellow romper, someone saw.

Lately there had been this dream, and Polly Talbot blushed just to think about it – a 68-year-old woman with long white hair and a wheelchair full of MS now, in the arms of a young man, their heads near a pillow. She had known this particular young man from the time he had arrived as a teenager for summers on the lake, and for years she had paid him for odd jobs around her island – repairing her dock, taking down dead trees, ramping all the entrances after she had her diagnosis. She was a practical woman. He was a capable young man. He was average and slender, with thick, gray blond hair and a quick grace. Soon he started taking jobs from other cottagers. *I've got to consolidate my position*, he told her, and he'd smile that smile, with his lips together, like it would give away too much to show his teeth.

When the dream started, all these years later, Polly realized she had spent years distracted by him when he was working around her place, stripped to the waist, clearing brush, chopping firewood. She liked it that he could keep up when she talked about the Italian Renaissance and wild orchids and Walt Whitman, all her special subjects. She suspected he had only a passing understanding of many things, but even that was charming.

Without telling him, she decided to leave him the cottage, because beside herself, no one had been the island's caretaker as much as this young man. He had studied commerce at McGill and now called himself a venture capitalist, so she believed he had a good head for property. Perhaps a cottage here would even consolidate his position.

Earlier that afternoon on the day of the regatta, Polly had wheeled herself out to the scrubby end of her island to watch the race as the sailors came through Wendigo Pass, the narrow channel between her place and the Wellers'. When she got there, she saw her young man's Laser rocking gently out in Wendigo Pass, the sail luffing. There he was, crouching, looking up the lake toward the finish line, and then in the other direction. She watched him sheet in and sail closer to the boulders snaking out from the Weller side, where he leaned over, jabbing again and again with a paddle, until he finally brought something up against the side of the boat.

Her hands flew to her open mouth when she realized what he had brought on board – it was the yellow romper that made it clear, even before she saw arms and legs – but she knew there was no one better to get help quickly than her young man. Polly saw him cover the little girl with his silver windbreaker to keep her warm where she lay out of sight at his feet. *Dear God, let him get help in time*, Polly thought, as she backed up her chair in the exquisite sunlight, turning for home, where she'd wait for news.

Hours later, she caught sight of him outside where she had wheeled to watch the race. He was studying the dirt path, scuffing at something with his bare feet. Pebbles, twigs, pine needles – still taking care of her, even on race day when it all meant so much to him, even at 32 when he was no longer a kid who needed a job. She knew he would come, because she had no phone.

And now he had.

She wheeled herself back farther into the great room of her cottage and reached for a book. The sun was low enough in the sky that it hit the water and reflected white ripples high on Polly's walls, and she watched him run softly up the ramp and try the glass double doors, almost as if he expected them to be locked. They looked at each other through the glass, and Polly smiled.

He came inside.

Just then she remembered the dream, the feel of him taking her into his arms, and spoke up just to cover her blush. "Why are you still wearing your racing gloves?" She said *still*. They both heard it. And she suddenly knew as she watched him roam around the room, touching her things with a freedom she had never seen, that so much depended on the word *still*.

She tried to work it out, but she was thinking how golden brown his eyes were, how wide his cheekbones, and how her father really should have bought the rocky island off the mainland, seventy-two years ago, instead of this one. He didn't because he he'd just plain miss good old dirt too much, he always said, the kind of good old dirt that preserves what were now his daughter's wheelchair tracks all those years later.

But what had she missed?

She should have taken Mo McCallum up on her offer to ferry her over in the blasted chair, bustled by strong arms and good-natured complaints up the hill to the decks. Someone would have called her the commodore, because her father had been, and someone else might have handed her the air horn to signal the start of the race. She could have joined them in the fake jeers at the skippers who couldn't keep their dinghies behind the invisible start line, the sound of the sails luffing in a sweet agony of anticipation.

There would be the usual commentary from Tom Fellows who owns the solar energy supply shop in Bracebridge, who always yells, *I've seen better Skippers in the Barbie Dream House!* and everybody laughs because they've waited for it all year. And there's Mary Dineen, who makes cream puffs every year for all the losers, although everyone shares. And Noah Trask, who cheers wildly for any kid in a Sunfish because he likes to see kids and the most basic boat in the whole wide world win.

She could have reached for the child Amy, who might even have crawled up with the butterfly book, remembering how Polly had given it to her because children remember these things, and Polly could have kept her safe from the baby jaguars that eat Blue Morpho butterflies. *But listen*, Mo McCallum had stopped reading when Amy went very still, *sometimes if it flutters its blue wings very hard and catches the sunlight just right, it blinds the baby jaguar just long enough to get away!* Amy's tiny finger tapped at the picture of the cat. *Amy*, said Mo, smoothing a hand over the wild yellow hair, *the baby jaguar is just a baby.* But even Blue Morphos get tired, and who is to say that the sun is just where you need it to be to manage those blinding flashes of blue no matter how hard you flutter in the warmth of the jaguar's breath? *Make no mistake*, she wished she could tell Amy. There in her silent cottage, with the reflected white ripples high on her walls, Polly felt his arm slip around her shoulders, the rough suede palm of the racing glove brushing against her light shirt, and she had no more dazzling blue in her to blind him. *Oh, make no mistake, Amy, even if your mother tells you that the baby jaguar is just a baby. The baby jaguar* – he nearly held her in his arms as she saw the bed pillow move in – *is still a jaguar.*

Two years later Steve Beck was sitting in his tent, waiting out the blowing snow, waiting out the dark that never really seemed to leave, even when the sun was a ragged blot in a milky sky. Beside him Carl Longo was curled on his side, asleep in his bag. Or was it Dean Cooper? Who had crawled in with him four hours ago? Cooper, Longo, Behrman, Henck, he'd climbed with them all, climbed down with them all, pulled each of them off mountains. Together they were called the Death Posse in mountaineering circles, who thought each of the five was a man just looking for a slightly more interesting way of killing himself.

Over shared flasks they all laughed kind of quietly about it. But none of them said otherwise. Cooper, he knew, had lost all of his mother's money in a hydrofoil scheme. Henck's brother was a paraplegic ever since an accident when Henck was drunk behind the wheel. About the others, Longo and Behrman, he couldn't say. *What'll it take?* they joked with each other, but only when they were climbing alone and not working as paid guides, because no one else would understand. *What'll it be, boys?* Forgotten crampons? A misjudged weather condition?

For himself, Steve Beck knew, but never offered to the others, it was the pursuit of the sweet crevasse. Something he had never seen before, beautiful in the shimmering daylight, deep in the profound night, cooling forever that gnarled overgrown thing that used to be his heart – a place to remind him of Mo McCallum.

And Amy.

He stirred, unzipped the tent door just enough to peer out at the snow that was white even in the dark, at the occasional star that stared back, even through the blow. He heard crunching, saw a headlight bobbling back toward where he knew the other tent must be – Behrman out for a pee. He rezipped the tent, the cold hardening around him like memory, and he could see the day in June two summers ago when he and the McCallums and Polly Talbot had met at the landing where he kept his little houseboat, since he couldn't afford a cottage.

The clouds were sleek in the early summer sky, the blue intense. He had just wheeled Polly onto the deck of his houseboat when Mo pulled up in her Subaru, Amy in her car seat in the back, a finger curled sleepily over her nose in the long drive from Toronto. He nearly jumped over Polly to kiss Mo and she laughed as his fingers swept over her eyes and nose and mouth, telling himself she was actually back, done with the business in town having to do with what they called the McCallum millions. *Hey, Squirt,* he said to Amy, who pulled her thumb out of her mouth and offered it to him.

While he loaded Polly's bags, and seagulls circled overhead, Mo sat right down on the dock with Amy in her lap, opening the little cardboard butterfly book that Polly had gravely presented. Amy's eyes were big and one of her soft little arms danced, the strands of many-colored bracelets catching the sunlight that was very nearly total.

He listened to Mo read that the Queen Alexandra's Birdwing butterfly is the biggest in the world, and the Zebra Longwing butterfly feeds on the nectar of passion flowers – *So do I,* said Steve, heaving a carton of canned goods on board, and Mo tried to trip him – and then there's the Peacock butterfly that hisses when it's scared, and Amy lurched, thumb in her mouth, at Polly, who cried, *Oh, he'd never hiss at you, not you.* Mo pointed to the next page: *Here's the Blue Morpho, Amy, and look at this, the Blue Morpho butterfly is eaten by baby jaguars. That's what it says.*

It had been pointless, finally, to try to reconstruct the tragedy, and they never – never – got past the first senseless five minutes after Rick Wakeman rowed Amy's little body to shore. All of the stupid, inadequate words were still clattering in his brain, which was no longer anything but an empty tin box.

Wakeman, Wakeman, I told you to tell her I was racing.

I did, goddamn it. Mo –

No, no, I don't remember –

You were standing right there. I told you Beck was racing.

Oh, my God, oh, my God.

Didn't you hear me?

I didn't hear you. Didn't you know I didn't hear you?

Mo, for the love of God –

Go away. Get out. You were supposed to be watching Amy.

Beck, maybe you'd better –

There is a kind of goneness that is so sudden and complete it was as if the child and the woman were pulled through a rift in the sky, just over the horizon, and the only thing left was for him to hurl all the rest in after them. His houseboat, his outfitting job in Cariboo, his furniture, his truck, his fucking tin box brain – and the Invitation, oh, yes. The Invitation went first. And even then all he had left was a gaping guilt that no altitude could refine out of him. He had turned his back on Amy and Mo that day just to play with the rich kids. That was what happened. Mo saw it plain. So did Rick Wakeman and the others. So, in fact, did he.

One thing remained.

One thing didn't get hurled through that low rift in the sky. He had found it, forgotten, on his houseboat, three days after Amy drowned, coming out of his stupor when Noah Trask had kindly come aboard just to clear away the empties and tell him that Mo had left for good. Half under his berth was the butterfly book Polly Talbot had given Amy when they all arrived on the lake just a few weeks ago.

He kept it, sewed it into his Osprey pack with a nylon patch cut from his old pack. He made the stitches small and ran the tent-sealing wax stick over them, hard, holding it like a knife, wishing he was carving out his own godforsaken heart. From then on he carried Amy everywhere with him, as small and present on his back as she used to be, and sometimes at night, cold in his tent before the goose down kicked in, he'd rest his hand on the small bulge in his pack, where he'd settled it by his head.

Steve could just make out Carl Longo at his side, rustling, and he knew daybreak was coming. He laced up his boots, unzipped the tent flap just enough to push his pack through to the outside. Hat, gloves, he set next to Longo. Those, somebody could bring down without too much trouble, and somebody could use. At ten thousand feet, at daybreak, the snow as far as he could see was rose-colored, like the mountain was bleeding into itself.

It wasn't much of a plan, but then it wasn't much of a life, and Steve Beck climbed softly out of the tent, the wind twisting through his uncovered hair, and zipped Longo back in as his fingers started cramping with the cold. He pulled the pack into place and felt Amy there between his shoulder blades. His cheeks were wind-ripped raw, and he was really past telling whether it was tears or flying specks of ice that stung, but he set out alone with Amy – he had her this time, had her good – to see if together they could find that sweet crevasse.

He relaxed against the leather seat in the back of the limo that picked him up every day from his office, and brushed at the creases in his Ferré pants. Rukhi the driver eased into Toronto rush hour traffic and headed up Bay Street. It was late April, warm enough to leave jackets behind but cool enough to hurry, a month away from going back to the lake, once the ice went out. People crowded the crosswalks, skirted by rollerbladers. He sat back and enjoyed the bicycle bells, the car horns, the neon. Anything that flashed and fluttered. At the intersection of Bay and Bloor, a young father with a blond-haired kid in a backpack joined the crowd, crossing. The kid had a yellow coat with a hood that had fallen back.

And he remembered Amy McCallum. Dead six years now. He didn't think about her very often – why should he? – but he found himself remembering regatta day on the lake in 2000. Mostly what he remembered was himself, how he saw it all in an instant – that he was going to let the McCallum kid drown.

Steve Beck had outsailed him, finding those slivers of wind all the rest of them missed, sensing the perfect moment to come about like it was written in water bugs on the surface of the water. Beck, in his scuffed-up Invitation he had bought cheap off an old cottager who no longer even took it out of his boathouse. Beck, who had met Mo McCallum somehow in Toronto over the winter, rounding her like just another marker, easing into their world on that lake whether or not he belonged. And then came the news, at cocktails at the Dineens' three days before the regatta. The wedding plans. Mo and Steve Beck. Sometime in the fall.

And he watched all his own careful preparations – over two long years – with Mo McCallum vanish. How he had circled her, kept her in sight, while he figured out she would dash if he moved too fast. He could tell by the set of her shoulders, by the slender muscles in her feet. So he settled on the dinners with her at Susur and North 44 in Toronto, bankrolled by his savings, drives in the olive-green MG convertible he had borrowed from his roommate Chad, and topped by the schooner cruise through the Carolina lowlands, after he talked her into leaving the brat with the nanny for five days. It was there he finally had her, had her good, every night in a row, keeping it easy, while he consolidated his position.

Then suddenly there he was on the Dineens' deck, there among the canapés and the seagulls and the shrieking pleasure of all the others, his heart no more than red coals caving into ash, having to shake Beck's hand, and kiss Mo McCallum's beautiful cheek with a smile so slash-like he thought his lips would part over his teeth.

He never gave her Beck's message that day when she was helping out in the Wellers' kitchen. *Could you tell Mo I'm going to race after all and can't watch Amy?* He didn't give her the message because he suddenly thought that deliberate oversight might lead somewhere interesting. And when he rounded Wendigo Pass, racing alone in his Laser, he took in two very separate sights that changed his life.

In the far distance he could just about make out the Invitation, becalmed near the final marker. Beck the frontrunner – Beck who had won Mo McCallum, Beck who in one month had delighted all the cottagers he himself had worked on for years, Beck who was the seat of every thwarted hope – had lost the wind. And near at hand he could see Amy McCallum all by herself, toddling over the rocks jutting out from the Wellers' island, bending, reaching for stones, reaching –

He could have called out to the kid, he could have swum to her faster than he could have reached her in the Laser, but he didn't because he suddenly saw as clear as the sky on race day that forces were coming together that he could summon. He was going to let her drown and he'd fix it to lay the blame at Beck's feet.

So he let the sail luff while he watched the kid spot something under-water – maybe a fish – and point it out to nobody, stump two little steps closer to it and tumble off the rock. She splashed only once and slipped under. The last he saw of her were loose yellow curls floating black from the weight of the water, then gone.

How long to give it? Two minutes? Five? Could he spare ten? Any minute some kids in a Sunfish would come rounding the bend into

Wendigo Pass and he had work to do. Nearly five minutes – it would have to be enough. He pushed the tiller to leeward, sheeted in and headed there on a beam reach. Then he grabbed his collapsible paddle to bring her up, pulling the body into the boat, and covering it with a windbreaker. One less complication in a life with Mo McCallum and the McCallum millions that was suddenly seeming very possible again.

He set a course through the pass, catching a glint of metal on the Talbot side, seeing old Polly wheeling herself back up the path. How much had she seen? He twisted away from her, mouthing Fuck to the sky, and kicked at the body with his bare foot. Then he sailed right for Beck, having to reach him and dump the kid overboard before Beck could catch the wind and beat him to the finish line.

As he closed in, he hiked out, away from the spectators cheering at the front of the Wellers' island. It was perfect, an ecstasy of risk, and nobody saw a thing when he tipped the body into the lake just twenty feet from Beck, who was distracted by the sudden wind he must have thought had abandoned him – like his luck. For how could Steve Beck ever explain to the grieving mother's satisfaction that he had sat there with not a goddamn thing to do for twenty minutes and not seen poor little Amy walk right into the lake?

"Rukhi?"

Two dark eyes met his in the rearview mirror, as the limo glided around the corner onto Yorkville. "Mr Wakeman?"

There was Mo McCallum up ahead, stepping out of the condo building right on time, her blond hair swirling up around her ears in the breeze, wearing a light camel coat that hung well over the shoulders he had always worried would carry her away. "Pull over up ahead, Rukhi," he said. "There's my wife."

She liked the lake in October because she didn't know it well. Birches yellowed, and the loons were rafting up to leave for the winter. The town, only ten minutes away by boat, felt as remote as the wind. The cottagers had all closed up and left for the year, so the work of seeming normal to these good people she had known all her life, which included her life before Amy, was done for a while. There was no one she could tell that the Mo McCallum they used to know was now making her home in the raven's *kruk,* or the silent whitecaps that had their own places to go.

It was simply what had happened to her when Amy died six years ago.

So much was spoken and so little made sense that it all just sounded like buzzing.

told you to
no, I don't
were standing
hear me?
know I didn't
Mo, for
supposed to be
maybe you'd –

After a time, she wasn't crushed, she wasn't even bedeviled. Something lifted her, finally, and she only pretended her feet touched the ground so that others wouldn't comment. Something made her continue to clothe herself because she realized she still had a form and needed to pay attention to those things. But she was now as diaphanous as the wing of a dragonfly and she had felt herself relocate to a place unreachable by all her old passions and sorrows.

She took the news four years ago that Steve Beck had slid off a mountain with that odd, concentrated airiness that filled her at those times and made her arms drift up from her sides. She couldn't call up any of the old warm presence of Steve Beck – it wasn't something within the powers of a thin, crinkling dragonfly wing – but she sat for a while at the Toronto waterfront and sent her mind out over Lake Ontario, as if she could connect with him somehow, just for a moment, in that place where all airy things collide and veer, without regret.

In the years since the regatta of 2000, Mo had placed herself at the head of the McCallum Foundation because a mere canister with a brain that was passing for human could at least get some work done. And she had. And she had married Rick Wakeman, finally, because he had a head for business and she could tolerate sharing her closets and bed and dinner table with him.

Mo puttered the sixteen-footer slowly around the shallows of what had been Polly Talbot's island. When Polly had died – her heart gave out the same day Amy drowned – and her estate finally settled three years ago, the cottage had come to Rick, and they were finally putting the place up for sale. Mo took on the job of deciding just what Polly's place needed, while Rick took out the Laser for one final sail of the year before they finished closing up their own cottage in the northern part of the lake, and leaving until next spring after the ice went out.

She had walked around Polly's island making notes into her digital voice recorder – *new flashing around the chimney, three fallen trees that have to be cleared, torn screens in the main cottage* – and now she was looking the place over from the water. The main dock was floating, probably dislodged ever since all the rain early in the summer when the lake reached a new high-water mark. Mo carefully avoided looking over at the sloping rock at the southeast point of the Wellers', where the spectators had stood during the regatta – and waited, later, while divers brought up Amy.

Even in the lee of the island, Mo felt the cold wind hit all the places she hadn't covered with fleece as she took the boat around the back of Polly's, near Wendigo Pass, where she checked out what was left of the old swimming dock. She shifted into neutral while she rambled into the recorder. *Beautiful setting here, lots of red pines, the rock kind of a natural waterfront. It might really be worth rebuilding the old Talbot swim dock, Rick.* While she talked she drifted, and the wind pushed her closer to the Weller side of Wendigo Pass. She was unfamiliar with the spot, couldn't read the shallows, what with the overcast, so she pulled up the motor and grabbed an oar in case she had to jab herself away from the rocks.

Then in a strip of cool October sunlight, the yellow birches on the Weller side of the pass shone. Light waves splashed the side of her boat and she heard the conversational *kruk* of a raven at the very top of a tall white pine. Pushed toward the rocks, Mo kept her oar ready as she watched the thin sunlight stream over the water, changing it from something dark and impenetrable – in the third week of October, a fatal 12° – to a place where she could see a fish dart and soft brown algae reach up from the bottom.

Not far from shore, maybe in four feet of water, something glinted. A lure on a broken line? It was blue. Mo leaned carefully over the side of the boat, trying to make it out. Rocks, boulders, sticks, algae. What could possibly be blue that had a place there with everything else? The sun continued bright, and Mo saw something else, strange and white, next to the flashing underwater blue. So many things, finally, are castaways. So many things are just dragonfly wings.

She took her oar and carefully drove the strange white thing over the submerged rocks, going back to snag the blue lure before she lost it down there in a cloud of disturbed dirt. Mo worked with the oar, teasing the white thing up to a place where she could grab it if she rolled up her sleeve. Then she pushed the oar slowly back over to the blue lure, twisting delicately to get under it before it sank between the rocks. She angled it finally onto the blade of the oar, which she levered carefully out of the water.

Her fingers lifted the lure.

Which wasn't a lure at all.

It was a bracelet, a bracelet of tiny blue metal beads.

On a thin elastic band.

The kind of thing a child might wear –

Amy.

She could see Amy, there at the landing – all of them, Steve, Polly, Mo, Amy – her eyes big, sitting in Mo's lap, dancing her little bare arms in the warm June sun, watching the play of the light on all the loose strands of many-colored bracelets while Mo read to her about butterflies and Steve loaded the houseboat.

Mo set the cold blue bracelet on the wooden seat, next to her, her fingers cramped like claws from fear and cold. Very carefully she took the oar, the chill starting at her wrists, a chill that had nothing to do with October, as she lowered the oar back into the water, heading right for the white object, which kept slipping off the oar, first to one side, then the other.

With a cry Mo tore off her jacket and plunged her arm into the lake, her other arm ramming the oar down between two boulders to keep the boat steady. She felt the thing tickling just a hair past her fingertips, but then she caught it between two fingers and tugged slowly against the water to bring it up.

What she held in her hand was a clear, plastic sandal.

Amy's missing jelly shoe.

Mo sank to the floor of her boat, her fingers trembling as she set the blue metal bracelet inside the shoe and held them long enough for the clouds to move in front of the sun, but not long enough to bring back Amy. *How in the name of God did they get here?* She placed them on the seat and stood up in the boat, gently rocking in the wind, looking around. Mo lowered the motor, pulled the cord, and headed farther into Wendigo Pass.

She looked at the place ten feet up from the water where Polly Talbot's path ended. *No, I'll just watch the race from my own land's end, dear,* Polly had said when Mo offered to ferry her over. And Mo could tell that from that spot Polly had a view of all the colorful sails as they came through – and Polly died sometime that afternoon. Did something alarm her?

Mo remembered the end of the race, when Rick had rounded the final marker, hiked out dramatically, underscoring his own win as he passed Steve and skimmed over the finish line. Steve came in second, followed by the rest of the sailboats, so close to each other that Tom Fellows yelled something about a school of Sunfish, and the crowd cheered while someone honked the air horn.

It was Rick who had sailed the race alone.

All the way.

Too far behind Steve.

Too far ahead of the others.

Alone through Wendigo Pass.

Amy's shoe and bracelet were in the shallows off the pass because – Mo turned the boat in a tight circle, staring at nothing – because that's where Amy drowned. How did she get to the final marker, where Steve sat, losing the race, losing it all? Did a current carry her, all that way, in three hours? It could, it had to, that's how it happened – but Mo knew the lake, and knew there was no true current, only fickleness, determined by whichever way the wind came over the water on any given day. So, how –

She slammed into neutral and staggered to her feet, seeing the rocks, the path, the Laser alone between them. The child, the old woman, the man alone between them. And as she staggered to her feet, she pushed her hands away from her face and looked down at herself. Herself. Mo McCallum. It was Mo McCallum that lay across the finish line that day. She howled into the wilderness of sun and water, and the birds rose crashing from the treetops, driven into the great true silences of her own ruptured heart.

Mo rode all the way back to their cottage with the throttle wide open, and pulled up rough alongside their own dock, where she tied up while she got what she needed and headed out again in the cold gray afternoon. She ran the boat fast over to Veil Point – nobody. Changed direction and cut across the waves to the secondary channel past the Dineens' island – nobody. Then she headed down to Fortune's Strait, another favorite sailing spot because there were no shoals.

There was the Laser.

A red starburst on a tall sail.

It helps to know a husband's habits, Mo thought as she idled, loading her dad's .410 double-barreled shotgun, then setting it beside her. The Laser was clipping along, and when it had reached a point far enough away from any island, Mo opened up all 25 horses and headed right for her husband, who was hiked out like it mattered, hiked out with the kind of extravagance he had needed the day he had pushed Amy overboard.

He started to scramble as he heard the boat approach, trying to see what was heading his way, but she announced herself by tucking the shotgun up tight under her other arm and blasting several good holes through the sail. At the last possible moment, she veered to the left, ramming his hull, and capsizing the sailboat. She had to work fast, pulling right up against the bow of the Laser, plunging her hands into the water to hook a tow line through the bow eye, and roaring off in her sixteen-footer, towing the sailboat out of her husband's reach.

While he cursed, sputtering, "What the fuck – ?" she did a tight turn, stopping not twenty feet away from where he trod water, and faced him. His eyes were wild as he tried to shake off the cold water – and when he realized it was Mo, Mo McCallum, his wife, his millions, and that a shotgun was leveled at his chest, he got very still and worked on sounding reasonable. "Mo! What do you think you – "

As he started to swim toward her, she blasted the water in front of him – he shrieked and hurled himself backwards – then quickly reloaded and snapped the barrel closed. She checked her watch. One minute, maybe a minute and a half, he'd been in. One hundred fifty-five pounds – it was comforting to know he weighed himself daily and always reported the results – in 12° water, how long could he last? Twenty minutes? Longer? Before he slipped under for good she wanted the truth out of him.

She switched on her recorder and held it up in her left hand. "Tell me about Amy," she shouted. "And speak up."

"I don't know what you're talking about."

"I found her shoe, in Wendigo Pass. And her bracelet."

A wave broke against his jaw. "Let me in the boat."

"No. First tell me about Amy."

"First let me in the fucking boat."

She was filled with regret. "Then tell me about Polly."

He nearly lifted himself out of the water with rage. "*No!*"

He kicked violently toward her. She blasted him back, watching the shot plink into the steely gray water, this time closer to him, nicking an arm. "Goddamn crazy bitch," he screamed, flinging himself onto his back to inspect his arm, shaking.

She held up a thermos – he didn't need to know it was empty – and pulled a toque over her head. "I have plenty of time, and you have – " she checked her watch again – "oh, eighteen, maybe twenty minutes – "

Then he started screaming for help.

"Seventeen minutes."

Then he started wheedling. Remembering sex, promising gifts, finally even offering divorce.

She sighed. "Sixteen minutes."

He choked, "Mo, for the love of God – "

"Tell me about Amy."

He started to cry. "Then will you let me in the boat?"

She lifted the recorder. "And speak up."

He jerked around, all the feral grace of him gone, bawling occasionally, swallowing water, choking it up, finally telling the story. How he had watched Amy fall into the lake, holding himself back, fascinated, bringing her up, drowned, on board, laying her off on Steve Beck –

He stopped, shrinking into the water, looking at her pleading, but she needed all of it, so "Fifteen minutes," was what she said. And he told her then about Polly Talbot, who saw it all there on the path. "She must have." He thrashed with sudden energy, his eyes ranging over the surface of the water, as if he could see it all right in front of him, maddeningly, when all he wanted was a hand up into the boat, a hand up into some understanding of his own motives that were now sunk among the rocks, forever out of reach. And Mo listened as he told her with quivering lips – could it be thirteen minutes already? – how he had come to her cottage later and smothered Polly Talbot in her wheelchair.

While he spoke, Mo watched a dragonfly land on the oar she had used to pull Amy's things out of the water. It twitched one of its wings and waited steadily for some admiration there at the end of the old season, when mosquitoes were scarce, and life was just a little harder. The man in the water was sobbing, huge shivering sobs, babbling about consolidating his position, and Mo recorded it all, her arm lifted, as she watched the cold October clouds slip sideways from the sun.

The dragonfly took off, past the crying man.

The sunlight caught it over the water, shining through the black and silver dragonfly darting over the whitecaps, to the overturned blue boat on an island nearby. Mo watched the man struggling in the water. He couldn't seem to open his eyelids wide enough, startling his eyes open again and again, as though he couldn't take in enough light.

She remembered Amy tapping at the picture of the baby jaguar, prowling after a Blue Morpho butterfly. Amy tapping. And for a bright moment Mo clutched her fleece jacket to her chest as though it held the child. Then she looked past the struggling man, reached into her pocket, and slowly pulled out her phone to call the police.   ⁂

THE NIGHT OF THE GREAT WIND

MICK SCULLY

In Chinese mythology the wind is Xian, the stealer of souls, who resides in the Black Valley beyond the great oceans. He is the greatest fear of sailors for they are easily taken. There are times when he rages ashore scouring the land for souls. The old, the sick and infants are easy prey. Those he takes have no hope of resurrection or peace, they will toss forever in turmoil among the waves of the Black Valley. He is the bringer of fear. No one can be easy when he is abroad.

In some stories he assumes the form of the dragon and travels inland breathing hot winds and fire.

The seventh of January 2005 was the night of the big storm. It was at its worst in the North of England. By mid-afternoon of the following day the streets of Carlisle were under eight feet of water; nine died, three thousand people were evacuated from their homes and the whole town was without electricity.

In Birmingham, which is without a major river, so it is only the drains and sewers that ever flood, there was not much rain, but the wind was ferocious.

In her flat on the sixteenth floor on the Druids Heath Estate Jean Boyce was in bed dying. Two floors below, in an empty flat he had just broken in to, Jimmy Slim sat hunched in the darkness, waiting to die too. Both heard the wind as it raged between the tower blocks hurtling the debris of the estate high into the air, smacking it against walls and windows, bouncing it off car roofs. Satellite dishes broke away from balcony rails and flags of St George, intact since last summer's European Championship, were taken and sailed away.

Dot Adams sat beside the bed of her sister, Jean, listening to the rasp of air moving in and out of her diseased lungs. Alf, Dot's husband, was away for a few days in Rotterdam on business, not an unusual event by any means. She was used to his trips away – usually to Holland. *Trips away*. Dot smiled at the phrase; in the old days there had been stretches in prison but he hadn't done time for years now. Too shrewd.

Dot had turned off the television at the end of the bed half an hour ago and now sat beside her sister in the darkness, listening to the wind outside and the ghastly shunt of air within Jean's chest that preceded each gasp for breath. Dot wondered if this was a gale, officially. She wasn't sure of the difference between high winds and gales, the two terms they used on the forecasts, but this, tonight, was strong enough to frighten her. For a fortnight now she had nightly watched pictures on television of the devastation caused in Thailand, India, Indonesia, by the Boxing Day tsunami and comforted herself that here in England we are safe from the vicious whims of nature. Now she was doubtful: perhaps it is true, you're not safe anywhere.

When she had called round this afternoon she had wanted to fetch an ambulance, but Jean had begged her not to. She didn't want to go to hospital, she wanted to stay here, in her own home. The District Nurse would be round in the morning. She would be all right till then.

So Dot had persuaded Jean to go to bed where she had made her comfortable. "I'll stay the night with you," she told her sister. "Alf's away. It makes no difference."

To the Chinese wind has a special significance. They distinguish between types of wind: cold; damp; hot; dry. But all are destructive forces, malign influences. In Chinese medicine, wind is regarded as one of the external causes of disease. Therefore, the execution squad, on its way to Druids Heath to seek out Jimmy Slim, were naturally uneasy.

Dot switched on the lamp beside Jean's bed. The pink light was useless for checking her sister's colour, yet there was no point using the overhead that filled the room with sickly yellow. She switched the lamp off, returning the room to darkness. Beyond the window bundles of black and purple clouds the colour of the worst kind of bruising scudded though the sky.

They both married villains, she and Jean. But there the similarity ends. Alf did all right. He concentrated on jewellery – became an expert, developed contacts. He joked that he was a more accurate valuer than any lah-di-dah who worked for expensive jewellers or antique dealers. And he was right. He traded in the raw materials too, gold, silver, uncut diamond.

Jean on the other hand had landed herself with Ray. He looked like a film star in the early days, could have had any woman he wanted, and he didn't turn many down. A good talker. Full of plans and dreams, a charmer.

But it all went down the pan. He was small time. Robberies, mostly on teams, but he did a bit of solo work. Mostly commercial, but a spot of house-breaking. One prison stretch after another. Alf wouldn't have anything to do with him work-wise, said he was a loser, that he was bad luck, and he was probably right.

His looks didn't last long. His health went. He died at fifty-four, without two pennies to rub together, of the same cancer that was now finishing his wife off.

Yes, Dot reflected, it was she who had got the better deal. A beautiful house, cars, holidays abroad three or four times a year, an amount of jewellery minor members of the Royal Family wouldn't turn their noses up at. While for Jean it was this shabby council flat stuck up in a hole through the ozone layer, barmaiding until her coughing got so bad they sacked her, then cleaning for a year until she couldn't go on. She's got bottle all right, Dot thought.

She looked at the luminous face of her gold wristwatch. Nearly midnight. She wondered what Alf was doing in Rotterdam. He'd take her anywhere she wanted for holidays except where he did business; so if she ever wanted to see the tulip fields she'd have to go alone, not that she was a great one for flowers.

She was going to miss Jean, she was a good sort, always cheerful and optimistic though God knows she had no reason to be.

In the big red room above the casino Hsinshu sat alone, his phone on the table before him. He was deaf to the sounds of the gambling below which drowned the noise of the wind attacking the city. His ears would only awake when the phone rang. This was his first test.

In this room, just a few hours before, the trial of Jimmy Slim had taken place. Hsinshu was still in his first year as Emperor of the Seventh Dragon. All twelve Barons assembled round the table, six each side, should see him for the man he was. His element was Metal. They must see and understand this. Hsinshu had sat at the head of the table listening carefully to all that had to be said about Jimmy Slim. Then he had risen, turned his back on the table and with his chin cupped in his hand paced a little, deep in thought. Considering. Coming to a judgement. All waited. He took his time. Then, when he was ready, he moved back to the top of the table, looked Jimmy Slim in the eyes, called him by his rightful name, Hsiaohai, and pronounced his death sentence.

Now in the empty room he was worried. He hadn't put a foot wrong since his take-over. He had run the Seventh with martial efficiency, adhered to and upheld the rightful codes, imbued his men with pride again and with ambition. Their domain had enlarged – considerably, their interests increased, their profits soared.

Jimmy Slim's treachery had given Hsinshu the opportunity to solidify his reputation – proving his metal. He heard again the silence, loud as a collective intake of breath, when he pronounced the sentence. Jimmy Slim held his head high, sullen and defiant, but Hsinshu saw the fear trickling in his black eyes.

They had stood over Jimmy Slim while Yangku went to alert the squad on stand-by downstairs. When they arrived Jimmy Slim jumped to his feet and marched away with them as if eager to have this over with. As if he were ready to meet his end honourably. Hsinshu had been pleased. It was as it should be in the Seventh. Now the little bastard had escaped, and he had three squads running round looking for him. This was wrong. It was not as it should be. It showed the rottenness that had been allowed to set in. The word of the Emperor should never be questioned, even by one for whom that word meant death, it was part of the Code.

Tonight the world around Dot had compressed into layers of sound like geological strata. The wind, louder and more powerful than anything else, formed the thickest layer, the noise of the objects it flung around formed a separate layer of discordant, erratic syncopation, Jean's breathing, harsh now and not unlike the barking of a dog, a further layer, and there were other sounds squeezed, trapped almost, between these layers: the screech of car brakes from far below; alarms sounding; the lift squeaking and clunking its way up and down the spine of the building; snatches of music from here and there.

She stretched out her hand and touched the turned sheet beneath Jean's chin. It was slimy with phlegm. She withdrew quickly, pulled a tissue from the box beside the bed and wiped her fingers. With another tissue she wiped Jean's mouth. Perhaps she should change the sheet. But it seemed cruel to disturb her. Not that her sleep was peaceful, the breathing was becoming louder, more desperate, her mouth gaping wide in its quest for air.

This was dreadful. She couldn't let her carry on like this all night. But what could the hospital do? Stick her on a trolley with a mask over her face pumping oxygen into her. For what? To extend her life by a few more hours, a day or two. Then through the raucous gasps there was a cry, near enough a scream, the body spasmed. Dot reached out for her sister's hand. "It's all right, love. I'm here with you. Dot." The body settled, the gasping continued as before. Gently Dot laid her hand on her sister's forehead. It was wet with cold sweat.

His name was Shuko which means bonebinder and he had no fear of the wind for his Element was Wood which is supple and can bend and sway with the vicissitudes of the wind. So the wind held no fear for Shuko. He knew that it is Metal that controls Wood which is why he had become a loyal and true servant to Hsinshu. We should know the powers of our energies but also their limits.

Shuko stood beneath a swaying fir tree listening with pleasure to its struggle with the wind. The needles of the fir branches whipped his face, but he would not move. He was like the tigress that for a thousand years stood guard at the South Gate. An opposing army fired a hundred arrows into her hide yet still she stood, her eyes blazing black and gold. If we cannot kill the tigress, cannot even make her fall, the army concluded, what hope have we of defeating her master, the Emperor. And so they retreated. Other forces disbelieving the story came as far as the South Gate, but seeing the tiger standing patiently, hearing the hundred old arrows clicking together in the breeze they took not one step further.

Shuko's eyes were fixed on the brightly lit doorway of the tower block a hundred yards away. Jimmy Slim was somewhere in that building. Shuko had followed him here. You are not the only Dragon with a powerful bike, Jimmy Slim. If you come through that door Shuko's gun is ready. Despite the words in his head Shuko hoped Jimmy Slim would not come through the doors. To use the gun, especially tonight in such a wind, would be unlucky. Water controls fire. Far better he stays there. When the squads arrive we will find him.

When Jimmy Slim had gone into the tower block Shuko had disabled his bike with Hokusai's *Great Wave* emblazoned on it. He had done this carefully without causing the beautiful bike any damage, It would be within the Code for Hsinshu to award this spoil to Shuko. If he did Shuko would change the colour from blue to green as is right for one whose element is Wood.

Shuko had phoned the squads with Jimmy Slim's location. Then he had phoned Hsinshu. One ring and he answered. His ears were waiting. Shuko had detected relief in Hsinshu's voice. It is not right for the Emperor to express gratitude for he has the right to expect service from Dragons, but Shuko heard, despite the roar of the wind around him, the sound of a relief so great that he knew it was gratitude Hsinshu was feeling towards him right then. Great things would follow this night's work, Shuko knew this.

Dot was in the kitchen having a cigarette and making herself a cup of tea. There was no drink in the flat. She wished now she had slipped a bottle of vodka into her bag before leaving home, but she had not known then she would be away so long.

Looking out from the kitchen window it seemed the wind itself was visible. The stripped winter trees twisted and contorted as if under torture, bent this way and in a second the other in the wind's force. Suddenly she laughed out loud for the story of The Three Little Pigs had entered her mind. *I'll huff and I'll puff and I'll blow your house down.* She saw pictures in her mind that must have come from childhood picture books, or had there been a film, Disney perhaps, of the wolf forcing clouds of breath from his mouth? Then the pictures were superseded by those of tornadoes, *twisters* they called them, didn't they? In America. On television programmes about disasters. They destroyed everything in their wake. She had seen cars lifted and flung around. Then beneath the roar of her own English wind she heard the steam from the kettle, the switch click off, the mad scratch against the kitchen window of the little pine trees in Jean's window-box, like the fingernail clawing of someone trying to get in. She popped a tea bag into a cup. Perhaps she should give Jean something to drink, but the task seemed impossible. She poured boiling water into the cup.

Crouched in a corner of an empty flat on the fourteenth floor Jimmy Slim could hear the wind too, but it was consumed for him by a greater noise, the repeating echo in his ear of Hsinshu telling him that the Code of the Dragons demands the death of traitors.

But he had got away, defeating not only the squad but also this evil wind that had fought him continuously as he rode his motorbike south from the centre of the city. It had taken all his strength and concentration to keep the bike stable, but he had done it. If he could defeat the wind then he could defeat Hsinshu. He repeated this to himself several times as if trying to engrave it on his consciousness so that it would become incontrovertible fact, a belief he could hold on to.

He knew they were out there looking for him. They had followed him as far as this estate but then he had woven in and out of the labyrinth of short streets and cul-de-sacs, whizzed like the wind itself round the tower block. His element was Water. Water is controlled by wind. He must not forget that. He must use this water energy tonight of all nights, then he might save himself. Now he repeated to himself: *My energy is the power of water. It has immense flexibility. It can move round, over, under, objects. It can absorb, wear away. It is the awesome strength of the great wave.* On Jimmy Slim's chest is a blue tattoo of Hokusai's *Great Wave*. His fingers reach in through his shirt and he touches it as he repeats the words. He thinks about the white man with the blue arm who did this tattoo, he died by fire. As a rule Jimmy Slim does not like white people, although he will fuck white girls if he wants, but he did like the strange young white man who made his tattoo. He did the small flame on his wrist too: the flame, sign of The Dragon. All members carry this sign. Black people Jimmy Slim did like. This is where his current problems arose. He got talking to Strombo last year at the dog track. It wasn't long before he knew most of the Doberman Crew. He liked those guys, the way they looked, the way they talked, very free spirits. It wasn't long before they were offering him little jobs, paying well and then offering even more for information about the Dragon's drug runs. It was how he got his bike. But was also how he got here.

Jimmy Slim remembered his first kill. The skinhead. The Code says the Dragon kills by fire and in Jimmy Slim's time that has always meant guns. Since Hsinshu became Emperor he has allowed knives and machetes because his energy is Metal. As he recalled his first kill Jimmy Slim reflected on the fact that perhaps his present predicament was inevitable. The power of his own energy was an irresistible force. Once the skinhead was unconscious he had taken him to the canal and dropped him in. Stood on the bank in the dawn light and watched the water do his work. He recalled the white face of the skinhead bobbing gently beneath the surface of the oily water.

A gust of wind struck the window of the flat on the fourteenth floor with such force that Jimmy Slim jumped, and felt sweat rise across the surface of his body. He did not like wind. This night was unlucky. Then he checked himself. *You are the power of Water. You can work with the wind. Go with it. Don't fight it. Wind and water. Against each of these Fire, which is the energy of the Dragon, is defenceless. In combination you will have the power to survive.*

Hsinshu rose and leaving his phone waiting on the table turned to face the dartboard which hung on the wall at the back of the red room. He focused on it. Meditated on his target. Then when he was ready he strode to collect three arrows. Standing ready before the target he placed his left hand inside his shirt to rest on the Chinese character for power that was tattooed in black in the lower jia, just beneath his umbilicus. He took his energy to his right hand. He breathed deeply, then threw the arrows. All three reached the House of Twenty simultaneously, and stood together in the board as close as Siamese brothers. Hsinshu smiled to himself; he was a true leader. And it was no surprise to him therefore that at that moment his phone began to ring.

Dot wished she knew more about the pulse. She had her index finger pressed against the radial artery of Jean's left hand. The pulse seemed very fast, banging away in fact. She knew from television dramas that you should count the number of beats in a minute. She glanced at her watch, but what was the point? She didn't know how many there should be.

Jean took another gasp. Her chest cracked, as if somewhere deep inside her a drawer was being banged shut. Then she lifted her head, was suddenly clearly awake. She grabbed Dot's arm and raised herself a little. "Why?" she gasped into Dot's face. "Why did you make me do it?" The effort was too much for her and her head flopped back onto the pillow, but she wasn't finished. "Twice," she managed to moan before closing her eyes and turning her head away from her sister.

Dot used a tissue to clean from her face the flecks of mucous that had flown out with her sister's words and discovered that she was wiping tears away too. She knew exactly what Jean was talking about. The *twice* left no room for doubt. She wiped her hands, rubbed another tissue over the face of her watch.

After all these years. Out of the sediment of their past. And these may have been her last words. Dot's own pulse was racing now and she recognised the urge to shake Jean, make her talk to her – about anything but that. Those should not be the last words Dot would have to remember.

It was the abortions. Of course it was. When Ray was inside, Jean used to have the occasional fling. She tried to keep them quiet but Dot was always able to wheedle it out of her. They were nothing serious until she met Derek Wilkes, a foreman at Longbridge. That went on for years. Twice Jean became pregnant and both times she had wanted to pass the child off as Ray's. But Dot wouldn't let her. She wasn't going to have Ray treated like that, left to bring up somebody else's kid, think it was his own, love it as his own. So she threatened to tell Ray everything she knew if Jean tried that one. Derek was married with a family and he wasn't going to chuck that over. So Jean got rid of them.

"I think you'd have left Ray for Derek if he'd have had you." Dot found she was speaking out loud to her sister. She expected no reaction to her words and she got none. Just the gasping. "Another good looking bloke, Derek. You always got the good looking ones." Often when Dot saw Gary Lineker on television she was reminded of Derek Wilkes. It was the smile. But there had been something special about Ray when he was young.

After all this time, and now right at the end, it was the abortions. *You made me.* It was true, she had. And perhaps it was wrong. But – and she tried not to continue the thought, but it was too late – if it was wrong, I've been punished, haven't I? Well and truly. Horribly. You never knew your children, well they weren't children at all. But Lee, he was nineteen. Nineteen. And Dot was sobbing. Reaching for another tissue.

To lose your only child at nineteen. God, if she'd done wrong, she'd been well and truly punished and so had he. She could not control her sobs and their noise deafened her to the sound of her sister's struggle for breath and the terrible wind beyond the window.

When Hsinshu had pronounced the sentence of death upon him Jimmy Slim was prepared. He knew the Code. The sentence was inevitable. Only a weak leader would have delivered a lesser penalty. He had felt no fear, was sure he would meet his end honourably. When the Squad came for him he did not hesitate, but rose to meet them. He noticed the crimson blindfold trail from Feiyang's pocket. It meant nothing. Jimmy Slim was ready to play his part in what was about to be enacted.

Then the great wave rose up in him. He jumped them at the car and made for his motorbike. He saw Shuko, the bonebinder, step from the shadows. He heard the shots he fired die in the wind. Jimmy Slim ran like the wind and he ran with the wind and when he reached his bike he rode in the same way, like a surfer.

Now though, sitting crouched in the darkness, he had become stagnant. He must resurrect his energy. Mental level. He must think before he acted. They had taken his phone, his gun, his knife. He had only himself. It was a phone he needed now. He had friends in the Doberman Crew, he had done good work for them. They could save him. Time was tight but they were clever. The black men could save him. They would like to wound the Dragon, destroy it if they could, take over the spoils. This could be their moment. That is how he should present it. If he had a phone he could call Strombo. They were clever, they could be here in minutes.

Jimmy Slim rose in the empty flat. There must be a thousand phones in this building. He looked out of the window. When he had arrived here the sky was black, now it was blue. A fierce, proud blue reflecting the light of the city. Then he looked down and saw the Squad's car crawling slowly towards the building. He saw Shuko, the bonebinder, step from beneath the swaying trees into the street light. The car stopped before him. The squad got out, and Jimmy Slim saw there was a back-up Squad coming to a halt behind them. Arched against the wind, their feet planted apart, their heads bent in close, they talked with Shuko. Then they straightened, turned to look at the tower. Moved towards it.

Dot couldn't get Lee out of her mind. Not that he was ever really far away from it. Alf seemed to have coped much better. Father and son were quite close when Lee was a boy but as he grew and became a bit wild there was a tension between them; Alf was always too quick to criticise, and Lee wouldn't stand for it.

The coroner had given a verdict of death by misadventure. But she knew it wasn't that. They said he must have got into a fight, or hit his head on something and then had fallen into the canal. No. Someone had put him in that water, she knew it. And she had lost count of the times she had prayed that whoever it was would pay for it, would meet a terrible end. Alf had used his contacts, even in the police, to try and find out what had really happened, but nothing came of it. Sometimes she thought she had learned to live with it, but she never would. Every so often something would happen to bring it all back, and the pain, and the desire for revenge, were as powerful in her as ever.

She tried to get her mind back on Ray, tried to see him handsome and smiling as he was when she first met him. She hadn't told Jean about him when she took her with her to the dance at the Unicorn all those years ago, this chap she'd seen about, so well-dressed, so good-looking, who smiled so nicely. If she had done would it have stopped Jean? Of course it wouldn't. As soon as she saw him she went for him. Though to be fair it was Jean, and not her, who Ray was interested in, right from the start.

Still, as things turned out… But perhaps with her he would have been different. Poor Jean. This terrible gasping was doing Dot's head in. She couldn't let it carry on like this. She must do something. The pillow, perhaps. It would only take a minute. The trouble is they might do an autopsy. Then she could be the one doing time, and longer than Alf ever did probably. But surely they wouldn't. The doctors knew she had cancer. She was only here because she wouldn't stay in hospital, wouldn't go to the hospice. Kept telling them she'd manage with the district nurses. Poor Jean. "You never did know when you were beaten, did you, love?" Dot told her sister.

It was moments like these that Shuko lived for. He would never be a leader, but as a loyal and true servant to Hsinshu there were times when he was able to assume his master's authority. This was such a moment. He stepped out from the cover of the fir tree and raised his arm. The wind thrashed at him but he stood firm as any tree or tiger and raised his arm in the headlights.

Shouting against the wind Shuko assigned tasks. He placed three men on the door. Three more would take the lift and work down from the top floor. Three would use the stairs in an upward sweep. They should take Jimmy Slim alive. Hsinshu did not want bullets left in the building. The two drivers should remain in their cars. If Jimmy Slim were to escape the building they should use the cars to kill him. Then Naokung, whose Element is Fire, shivered in the wind and stepping back looked upwards at the tower block. He laughed suddenly and loudly as those whose predominant energy is Fire are prone to do when taken by surprise, for he had seen the silhouette of a figure in a window two floors from the top.

Jimmy Slim, energised now to violent movement, had to rise: it is the nature of Water under pressure, rise first, spread, fall. He sprinted the steps to the top floor, booted the first door he saw. It shook against his force. Booted again it flew open and sagged against the wall. Jimmy Slim surged through.

Dot thought it was the wind. Perhaps the whole building was coming down. Recent images from television of hotels and beach homes being washed away swept through her mind. She jumped to her feet. She must escape. She made for the bedroom door. Jimmy Slim saw the black corridor open into blue like a subterranean channel of clear water. He made for it. It could have been a sea creature, but it was a fat old woman he met in the doorway. He saw yellow hair, grey painted lips. Dot screamed when the male shape surfaced from the darkness. Jimmy Slim took her by the throat. In his grip he walked her backwards into the bedroom. In the lesser dark he could see the glint of rings on the hands that tugged at his. He could hear her panting into his face.

He flung her down onto the bed. Released from the collar of the man's fist Dot opened her mouth to scream again but only a stifled gurgle made it out into the room. She felt Jean's head beneath her back, dentures sticking into her. Above her stood the young man. Thin. Not very tall. But his anger and strength were greater and more dangerous than the howling wind outside.

"Where's the phone?"

Dot heard his words, or heard words, but they made no sense. She was swamped by his presence. His violence. This man was going to kill her. She had no doubt. Would he rape her first? She hadn't the strength to resist.

He reached out and pulled her up towards him. "The phone," he bawled in to her face. "Where's the phone?"

"In the other room. Through there." He flung her back, and as he did so a new darkness instantly descended.

The lift stopped between the tenth and eleventh floor. The three men inside, poised and ready for action, were consumed by a shocking still blackness. Everything had stopped.

In the stairwell Shuko cursed as the darkness fell. He cursed in Chinese. His curse was echoed by the other men. He would not be defeated by this. Naokung had seen Jimmy Slim on the fourteenth. They were now between the third and the fourth. Jimmy Slim could not use the lift. They merely had to continue to rise. He held on to the metal bannister for guidance and calling to the others to follow continued to climb.

For the three men suspended in the dark at the centre of the tower block this was an impotent agony. They tapped the sides of the lift, located and pressed at the useless buttons. There was confusion. This building was bad luck. Where was the emergency power? A generator. There was irritation. This building was useless. A shit-heap. Then anger, then fear as they simply had to wait without direction or knowledge hanging in the dark.

Jimmy Slim looked out from the window on the sixteenth floor and saw all the tower blocks were in darkness. A few headlights snailed away in the underworld below, but the sky was black and empty, occupied now by nothing but the wind. It was pointless searching for the phone, it would be dead too. Behind him the woman on the bed seemed to be crying. He smiled to himself. This wind may yet prove to be his saviour.

Now in these moments of reprieve for Jimmy Slim the greed that was one of the flaws in his character asserted itself. He had seen the rings on the woman's fingers, the gold wristwatch, the pearls around her neck. Spoils you don't turn your back on. They may not be as valuable as they looked. What would they be doing in a place like this? But Jimmy Slim would trust his instinct. Old women were funny, they often held on to valuable items despite the circumstances in which they lived.

He has started to undress me, Dot thought as Jimmy Slim pulled up her head and unclasped the pearls. Then he slid the rings from her fingers, removed the gold watch from her wrist. The room was full of her gasping breaths. It was not until he said "Where's your money?" that she realised she was being robbed, not raped, and found her strength. "I haven't got any money. I'm just visiting – " Jimmy Slim hit her. "In my bag. In the kitchen."

There was no point stumbling around trying to find the kitchen, then the bag, just for a few pounds. He had the jewellery. Now he must get out of here. Back out into the wind.

He found the stairwell door easily enough. Tugged it open with confident ease. He felt for the bannister rail and started to descend, and as he did so he could hear the rings tinkle in his pocket, a louder sound it seemed to Jimmy Slim then than the whip of the wind beyond.

When Shuko heard the door open he stopped dead and listened to the descending footsteps. The men behind him did the same. Silent. Motionless. Hardly breathing. The Dragons stood listening to Jimmy Slim coming towards them in the dark. He stepped straight into Shuko's arms, and gasped his shock. The lights came on. A dim blue light showered the stairwell illuminating for Jimmy Slim his fate. Distantly he heard the chug of the lift resuming its ascent.

They took Jimmy Slim back in to the empty flat on the fourteenth floor. An hour ago it had been Jimmy Slim's dark haven, now it was full of the shadows of men. Shuko was outside on the phone to Hsinshu. When he came in to the flat he took the crimson blindfold from Feiyang, but he did not tie it round Jimmy Slim's head as Jimmy Slim expected. Winding it round his fist he made a mitten of it and used it to protect the window lever from finger prints as he thrust it upward. Jimmy Slim understood now.

The wind roared in and filled the room. It may have knocked Jimmy Slim from his feet had his legs not been grasped by Yihsi and Naokung. Feiyang and Shuko took him at the arms, and all four men lifted Jimmy Slim up and hauled him through the open window out into the waiting wind.

As Jimmy Slim plummeted through the air Hsinshu was downstairs in the casino. He had just lost money on number fourteen. Shuko's call had distracted him. He had changed his mind at the last minute. Then he smiled. It was not such a bad thing for him to be seen by the punters losing money on the roulette wheel with good grace. It showed that we are all subject to fortune. 〰

THE RAINBOW KILLER

GARY W. SHOCKLEY

Gloria Whiting plucked the fabric of her dress away from the small of her sweaty back as she lugged her suitcase down the shabby hallway. She felt tired, sticky, and constipated after the long flight from Los Angeles and the bumpy cab ride into Houston's southside. The cabby had been alarmed when she told him to pull over ("Lady, you sure you know what you're doing?"), and now she was booked into room 14 of a sleazy hotel in a bad part of town.

She half-dragged her suitcase down the garbage-strewn hallway. The fluorescents were broken, filled with web, and the numbers on the battered doors were barely readable. A deep knife gash ran along the wall, zigzagging to a frenzy of deep stabs in a door. To her relief, it was not hers. As she listed onward, she saw a slender black man in a white uniform dipping his way toward her, in rhythm to some internal song. At first she took him for a janitor, but his uniform wasn't all that clean, nor was he. In addition to his rhythmic dip, his whole body shook. She suspected his dipping motion was an attempt to hide it.

"Hey, Princess," he half-sang. "Do me a favor? Check the girlie room for me. Tell me there ain't somethin' written in the stalls." He pointed to the women's restroom. "Somethin' in big fluorescent orange?"

She glimpsed pock-marked cheeks, yellow-tinged eyes, and a skull-and-crossbones earring as she ducked past him.

"Excuse me, Princess. Didn't mean to wrinkle your nose."

As she rushed to unlock her door, she saw him hesitate next to the women's bathroom, then dip onward.

The room was ten by ten feet. Locking the door, she dropped her suitcase and collapsed on the small bunk bed. The stink of mildew filled her nostrils. A shoestring dangled from a bare bulb in the ceiling. It twitched as a fly repeatedly landed and took off from it. She reached up and tugged. The room barely woke from shadow. A small desk with two legs missing hunched next to the shuttered window. She imagined herself petting it as she edged toward sleep.

High-pitched cries brought her to her feet. She tugged down a slat in the blinds and shielded her eyes. The midday sun beat relentlessly down through the smog. Several noisy kids cooled off in the spray of a fire hydrant. She stared at a rainbow scintillating in the spray, feeling for a creative spark in her, a desire to be active once more... The slat snapped back as she released it. Collapsing on the bed, she pulled off her blonde wig and scratched the brown hair beneath. Then she used a Kleenex to wipe off most of her makeup. She considered washing, but there wasn't a sink in the room. She would have to use the shared lady's bathroom in the hallway. She lay there, worrying the pendant on her necklace, and realized she was too tired to care.

She woke drenched in sweat and hungry despite the heat. It was four in the afternoon. The women's bathroom had no toilet paper, and the water in the shower was rusty and lukewarm. Despite the heat, she put on makeup, donned the wig again, and slipped into one of her more stylish outfits, an aquamarine dress with black lace.

She found a McDonald's three blocks away. The clientele was working-class Hispanics, Asians and Blacks, with a smattering of out of work and homeless. Tattoos were everywhere. Pungent sweat mixed with the acrid smell of asphalt, fiberglass, paint, and diesel fuel. She sat down in a corner booth to eat a chicken salad and read the paper. A small headline on page two caught her attention: RAINBOW KILLER STRIKES AGAIN. She skimmed the text: 'The Rainbow Killer struck again, if residents in the South Park district are to be believed. What's known for sure is that three people were killed, a dozen others injured, and four arrests were made–'

A shadow fell across her, and a Big Mac and coke settled onto the table.

"Well, if it ain't the Princess."

She watched as the black man from the hotel hallway dipped into the seat opposite.

"Nice outfit," he said, fingering her sleeve. "But McDonald's? Eating alone? These are hard times. Hard times indeed." He laughed. "The name's Shakes." He held out his hand. It shook. "You got a name?"

She ignored his hand. "Princess."

He laughed for some time at that, exaggerated guffaws that drew everyone's attention. "Princess indeed." He wiped his brow and grimaced. "It is hot. Hot hot hot. LA this hot?"

She tensed, wondering how he knew where she was from. It occurred to her he could have glimpsed the airport tag on her suitcase. She took a bite of salad.

"But you, Princess. You're cool. Yeah. Real cool. Tell ya what I'm gonna do. Seein's how you're new in town, short on company an' all, and how I happens to got me some spare time, what say I show you the town, make a night of it, see?" He laughed.

She sipped her Coke. "Could you be more specific? Are we talking opera or ballet?"

"Opera? Ballet? Sheee-it. I'm talking more like – " his eyes got big for a second " – the Bloodbath Theater. Wait wait wait, now hear me out. Sure, they got roaches, but they keep 'em on leashes. And tonight – well, tonight's triple-feature night." He took a large bite of his sandwich.

She watched him chew. "What time will you pick me up?"

He choked and wiped his face with a napkin. He stared at her. "Uh, starts at eight, you know, so – " He clapped his hands, and everyone looked his way. "Damn! What am I thinking? I got some shit ta do tonight. Prior commitments, you know?"

"You were expecting me to say no, weren't you."

He delivered more long guffaws, interleaved with sharp intakes of air.

"You wanted me to say no," she persisted, "so you could go off telling yourself what a stuck-up white bitch I am. It would reaffirm your contempt for well-educated, upper-class whites. That's your game, isn't it. Hating people like me. That's how you get your kicks."

"Awh, shit," he said, getting up and dipping away. "You're a crazy fucking bitch, you know that?"

"Oh, by the way," she called after him. "A message from the stalls: 'The pot of gold corrupts the Mother Lode.'"

He stopped and gaped at her, neck twitching, mouth half-open. "Fluorescent orange?"

She nodded. She had found it in the second stall at the hotel.

A police officer entered the restaurant and stared at Shakes. Shakes started dipping backwards toward the exit.

"When will you pick me up?" she called to him.

He looked from her to the cop while pushing out through the door. "Yeah, sure. Seven-thirty, make it. Seven-fucking-thirty."

At seven-thirty he came for her. He had made a gallant effort to groom himself. His face looked washed, but worse for it. And his pants and shirt looked clean, though old and badly wrinkled.

"Uh, we'll have to walk," he apologized. "Cars and me don't get along. Tend to forget I'm driving. The police, they recommend I don't, you know?"

"That's fine."

He looked her over. "Uh, maybe you could dress down a bit. Casualize, you know."

She had not changed since McDonald's. "I thought you liked my dress."

"Yeah, well... Yeah. Yeah, sure. That's fine." He clapped his hands nervously. "Fine, let's go."

As they walked down a garbage-strewn street toward the theater, she asked him what the graffiti was all about.

He dipped and shrugged. "Some dude I don't like. Had myself a good janitor job couple months back. Lost it 'cause of him. Boss told me to stop the graffiti. No can do. Not with Fluorescent Orange working the stalls. A cross-dresser, he is. Or she. Hits boys and girls bathrooms both. Worst serial graffitist this city seen. But I'll catch him. He keeps dropping clues. 'A pot of gold corrupts the Mother Lode'. See? He's a miner, works in a jewelry store. Got a hang-up on his mom. I'll catch him. Someone's gotta. 'Cause he ain't just got a mind to hurt me. No. This guy's a maniac. Yeah, I can feel it. He's dangerous."

"Like the Rainbow Killer?"

A sly grin crept onto his face. "Shit. You don't believe that crap."

She shrugged. "Who knows what to believe these days?"

The Bloodbath Theater was a PROGRESSIVE ENTERTAINMENT CENTER, as stated beneath the marquee. Several lawn sprinklers were rigged to the ceiling, and every time a bloody scene appeared on screen, fake blood spewed across the audience. Protective plastic garments and goggles were available to those wanting them. Gloria and Shakes both donned them. The triple feature consisted of *Panic in the Seats*, *Wince is Not Enough*, and *Leave it to Cleaver*. They stayed for all three, getting out at midnight. Out on the street, Shakes turned critic.

"Blood don't look like that, no way. Not that red. Don't spray like that either. It spurts. You know, in time with the heart. And those weren't real intestines. Roxie – she's my late wife – when she got gutted, they was whiter, looked like spaghetti spilling on the floor. Say, you hungry? I know a real good Italian place stays open till two."

She took a deep breath to fight down her queasiness. "No, I'm fine. About your wife – did they find who did it?"

"Oh, it was me. Don't worry. I'm rehabbed. Ten years in the pen. Five years of counseling shit. Hardly think about doing things like that no more."

Gloria took another deep breath. "Your wife must have done something terrible to provoke you like that."

"Nope. I just kinda went berserk. We're watching the cartoons, see, and then I'm standing there with a butcher knife going to town. Total fuckin' freak-out. Spaghetti on the floor. Rehab time. Say, we could eat Thai. Kanomwan's good."

She shook her head. "No food, please."

"Shakes!" someone shouted nearby.

"Honker, my man!"

Gloria watched as Shakes exchanged a complex handshake with a chubby black man, who gave her a suspicious look.

"She's cool, Honker," Shakes said. "She's cool."

"She the type makes you wanta think she's cool."

"Honker, you just jealous. We went to the Bloodbath. Shit, she loved it."

Gloria met Honker's fiery gaze and did not blink.

"What you want with Shakes?" Honker said. "What you setting him up for?"

"Shakes is showing me the city," she answered.

"Yeah, Honker. It's a fucking date, see? And I'm showing her the city."

Honker shook his head and started off. He cast back, "Shakes, when you remember you're black, drag what balls you got left down to Ja Ja's. Crazy muthafucka – "

"Fucking paranoid!" Shakes shouted after him.

"It's okay," Gloria calmed him. "You can't expect him to trust a total stranger."

"Yeah, well, he's a stranger to me, now on. Muthafuckin' mutha-fucka."

"What's this Ja Ja's he mentioned?"

"Just a hangout," he said. "Nothin' special."

"I wouldn't mind hanging out a while," she said.

He laughed out loud at that. "Not with these cats. They ain't your type."

"What *is* my type?"

"This ain't."

"But you hang out with them."

"Yeah, yeah."

"Then they're my type."

He stopped and picked up a chunk of concrete. He hurled it through a window. "What the fuck you want with my type anyway?" He threw another chunk. "What you want from me?" He threw a third chunk.

She winced at shattering glass. "I – I want you to show me the town – like you said you would. Your town."

Twelve blocks west, they ducked down some steps under a strip joint. The ground-level windows were boarded up, and the door was wall-papered with a black-brick pattern. Shakes knocked lightly, then opened the door. They entered a small foyer whose walls were covered with street signs. Music, voices, and a harsh clacking came from beyond a beaded curtain. Shakes parted it, and Gloria stepped through.

The room was dark, lit by purple Chinese lanterns and a large flat-panel TV on the wall. She choked. A Casablanca fan, slowed by small objects dangling from the blades, barely cut the marijuana haze. Gangsta rap pulsed in the background, obliterated by the clash of skateboards as two teenagers fought with them like swords. One almost hit her.

"Hey, man!" Shakes said, grabbing the skateboard. "Watch the Princess."

"Oh yeah?" The teenager jerked it free and held it up threateningly.

"Onus. Slick. Take it outside," said a large Chicano with a spidery eyepatch.

"Awh, man, we ain't doin' – "

"Take it outside!"

They left grumbling. Even as the beads settled, Honker pushed in through them. He gave Shakes and Gloria a nasty look, then squeezed past and settled on a sofa.

Gloria looked about. Two people sat on a second old sofa, five more were playing poker around a card table in the back, several more were sprawled on the floor. All were male. Most had been watching a boxing match on TV. But right now she felt herself the focus of attention.

"She's cool," Shakes told everyone. "She's cool, really."

"Shakes," someone said out of the smoke. "You pimping these days?"

"She – " His shake got worse. He swallowed hard. "She ain't that type, Milo."

"Come on, Shakes. Give us a stab at her. We'll tell ya what ta charge."

"You watch your face, Belly!" he said, pointing a stern finger at a heavy-set white man lotused against the wall. "She's – " he hesitated " – a good friend o' mine."

"Shakes. You ain't got no friends."

"Maybe it's his sister."

Everyone laughed.

"Go fuck yourself." Shakes hooked her arm and led her over to where Honker sat. "Mind if we join ya?"

Honker scooted aside, pretending to be intent on the boxing match. Gloria sat at the opposite end of the sofa, with Shakes in the middle. She shifted about to avoid springs pressing up through the cushion.

"Shakes," Belly said. "Least you could do is offer the lady a drink."

He jumped up. "Uh, yeah, Princess. Want some refreshment?"

"Re-fresh-ment," Milo said, amused by the word. "Re-fresh-ment."

"A beer would be fine," she said.

As Shakes headed for the kitchen, several new people entered and went in a back room. Others emerged and left. They did so as inconspicuously as possible, casting suspicious looks her way. She glanced aside at Honker, still intent on the fight. "You followed Shakes and me here," she said to him.

Honker gave her a peeved look, then shifted over close to her. "Let me tell you 'bout Shakes and me. See, we were pen pals, a dime's worth. Watched each other's back. Still do." He grabbed her hand and placed it on his side.

She felt a gun.

"I wouldn't want nothin' bad happenin' to Shakes. See?"

"I wouldn't either," she said. "But suppose something did. How would you go about killing me?"

He glared at her.

"Would it be execution style, one or two shots point blank to the base of the skull? Or would you just blast away at my heart?"

He gave her a hard, waffled look, then stood up. "You don't read right, Princess. You watch it, or I'll do worse than you can imagine." He walked back to join the card players.

"What was that about?" Shakes said, returning with two beers.

"Honker just wanted to know if I needed anything."

"Nah nah nah, that ain't Honker. Whatever he said, don't pay him no mind. He just jealous."

A rap song ended and another one started. More people entered and left the back room. "Business," was all Shakes would say about it. Most were Black, with some Chicanos and Asians. Once she heard angry voices coming from there, but no one seemed to pay it any heed.

One card player caught her attention. Mustachioed and Hollywood handsome, he was dressed in an oversized jacket with a yellow shirt and a red tie. He tipped his white panama hat to her and smiled.

"Shakes," she said, "who's Mister Color Conscious over there?"

"Oh, that there's Duke. Used to be on *Soul Train*. Dude can dance, that's for sure. Good with the chicks, too. He'll hit on you 'fore the night's out." He gave her a sincere look. "Hey, you wanna leave with him, that's your business. I understand."

"What makes you think I'd want to leave with him?" she said. "You think he's better than you?"

"Shit no. Just that, you know..." He let it fade out.

A weaselly black man shuffled out of the shadows, carrying a small sack. He hit a wall switch, and the Casablanca fan began to slow.

"Awh, Loon! Don't do that! It's fuckin' hot!"

"Goddammit, Loon! Turn it back on!"

Loon paid them no heed. Gloria now saw that the objects hanging from the blades were Ken and Barbie dolls. Loon climbed up on a chair and started stringing more dolls to the blades.

"That's Loon," Shakes said to her. "One time he built a time machine out of milk cartons. It worked. Problem was, we couldn't move more than five or six seconds forward or back. He should've used the plastic gallon jugs." Shakes toasted the fan with his beer. "Now he's playing with them dolls. Been doing it a month now. Says he'll bring back Elvis. No musical taste, Loon. Should bring back Notorious BIG."

"Hurry up, Loon! I'm turning it back on!"

The beads parted, and a tall black man entered, cursing under his breath.

"Ja Ja, my man! Where you been? You missed the fight."

"Muthafuckin' po-leece," he said, peeling off his shirt. "You believe that shit? I – " He stopped to look up at the fan. "Awh, Loon! Jesus! It's an oven in here!" He cursed a moment longer, then resumed. "Yeah, man, I was walkin' down the middle of the goddamned street, minding my own business, and the po-leece put me down, give me the spread. Believe that? Shit, no one usin' the goddamned street." He held up his wrists. "Cuffed me good, those muthafuckas. Down to the station. In-ter-ro-ga-tion. Two fuckin' hours. What the fuck for?"

"The way the System works," someone said. "Cops want us small fry, 'cause we easy game."

"Lazy sons of bitches," Ja Ja grumbled. "We oughta – " He paused, staring at the traffic in and out of the back room. "Hey. Hey! What's that shit?"

"Mamba's unloadin' some stuff," Milo said.

"That fuckin' moron! Why's he doin' that here? Shit. Loon! Hurry it up! We're sweating like pigs! Jesus."

"Us small fry," Belly said. "Police go after us 'cause they afraid o' the real muthas. That strangler in the Cloverleaf, how many he got now? Six?"

"And slice-and-dice on the docks. He's been cutting up whores a year now, they care?"

Gloria leaned forward and cleared her throat. "What about the Rainbow Killer?"

Everyone looked at her, including Ja Ja. "Who the fuck's this?" he said. "Just *who* the fuck is – ?"

"Shake's chick," someone said.

"Yeah, she with me," Shakes said. "She cool."

"She with you, Shakes?" Ja Ja's expression turned incredulous. "And you say she's okay? Shakes, you ain't got a fuckin' – !"

"She's okay," came a deep voice. "I know her."

Gloria looked for the speaker. He was the colorful card player, the one Shakes called Duke.

"You know all the chicks, Duke," someone complained.

"And not all o' them's cool," Ja Ja said, continuing to glare at her.

"I know her too," Honker finally said from the card table. "She's okay."

Ja Ja looked at Honker and then back to her. "What the fuck's goin' on around here?" He tromped to the door in the back, opened it and slammed it behind him.

Gloria glanced back at Duke, who tipped his white hat to her. Then she asked, "Is the Rainbow Killer real?"

Milo chuckled and lifted himself out of his chair. He walked dramatically over to the sofa, put a foot on its arm, and leaned over her.

"My brother really dead?" he asked. "Hey, Rin Tin. Your aunt and sister. They really dead?"

A black man wearing a yellow bandana on his head gave her a hard look.

"Diddy. What about your cousin? And Rico. Your – ?"

"Lay off, guys," Shakes said. "She just in from the West Coast."

"I don't care if she's from the North Pole! It's none of her fucking business."

"West Coast?" Rin Tin said. "Hey, mahn. We got ourselves a California girl."

"Where's her surfboard?"

She ignored their comments. "Is he real?"

"Make-believe," said one of the card players.

"You don't know fuck, Deadhead," Milo said.

"You ever seen the guy?" Deadhead countered.

"Shakes did. Didn't you, Shakes."

Shakes squirmed. "Come on, guys. You know I ain't never seen 'im."

"Just a matter of time. 'Cause you're way overdue at the Brick."

"The Brick?" asked Gloria.

"Gulfton Ghetto's worst tenement. That's Shakes's pad."

"Come on, guys," Shakes said. "I'm trying to watch the fight." But he wasn't even looking.

"So. Who exactly is this Rainbow Killer?"

Milo gave her another hard look, then tilted his head back and crooned, "Some-where, o-ver the rain-bow."

"Tha's his song," Deadhead shouted over him. "A big muthafucka, three maybe four hundred pounds. Walks easy-like, all relaxed, out for a stroll in the park, and he's singing that song. Only he's got an axe. Carries it like a briefcase. Yeah."

"And it's dripping blood," Rin Tin said.

"Awh shit, Rin Tin. There ain't never been blood around. Not from his axe, anyway."

Several more had joined in the song. The rest argued about the axe. Some thought it left a trail of blood. Others didn't think he carried one at all.

"Hey, Princess," said Milo. "Maybe you get lucky and meet him on the way home."

"Shit, going home's the safest part," Deadhead said. "It's once you're there you gotta watch out. Ain't that right, Shakes?"

"There ain't no Rainbow Killer," said Shakes, sinking deeper into the sofa.

"Yeah, right," said Milo. "That's why you don't sleep in the Brick no more."

Several people laughed.

"Don't like the bedbugs is all," he grumbled.

"Take our advice, Princess," said Milo. "Go back to La-La Land fast as you can, 'cause nobody's safe around here, not from the Rainbow Killer."

Gloria leaned close to Shakes. "You okay?"

"Fucking make-believe," he quivered. "You think I'm afraid of him? Goddamned Rainbow Killer can't even make hisself real."

"Nobody's seen him all that clear," said Rin Tin. "Never know, maybe he's just a midget in the end."

"Might be at that," said Deadhead, "'cause he don't do the actual killing. He's just a bad influence. A fucking bad influence."

"Puts evil thoughts in your head."

"No, no, he don't put nothin' in! It's already there. He just helps pull it out. That's what happens when he's around. You do what's deep inside."

"Yeah, and you know what that means, Princess," Milo said. "Shakes here, he Deep Red himself. Bad company, Princess. Ba-a-a-a-d company."

"Come on, guys," Shakes said. "I ain't like that no more. I hardly ever think bad stuff now."

"It's still in there," said Honker. "You just buried it deeper."

"The killings, though," Milo said. "The ones Mister Rainbow Killer facilitates. They ain't normal. They're bigger than life."

"Spectacular."

"Supernatural."

"Yeah, that's the word. Supernatural."

The singing intensified, some people humming, others whistling, some mumping at the lyrics.

"Christ, Soup. Learn the words!" someone said.

Even Gloria joined in, her well-trained voice resonating above everyone else's.

"Hey, the chick's got lungs!" Rin Tin said appreciatively.

"Shhh!" someone said.

Everyone fell silent. A whistling came from outside, following along.

"Oh come on," Rin Tin said. "The Rainbow Killer ain't a whistler. He got a voice."

"Oh? You heard him, Rin Tin?"

"I know people have. He got a real deep voice. Sings off-key, too, and he don't know all the words."

People started singing again. Gloria saw that Shakes had sunk deeper into the sofa.

At last Loon finished with the fan. No sooner had his hands cleared the blades than Milo hit the wall switch. A collective sigh rose. Loon sat down in the chair and stared upward at the spinning dolls.

"Hey, Loon. What you think of the Rainbow Killer?"

Loon slowly unfocused from the fan and looked about. "Don't exist," he said. "Just a cartoon."

"See? Even Loon don't buy it."

After a third beer, Gloria excused herself to use the restroom. There was only one, off to the side of the tiny kitchen. It smelled of piss, and she had to wipe off the seat before using it. Looking about, she saw crude graffiti scribbled over everything within reach. As she finished, she glimpsed a fluorescent orange scrawl down low behind the toilet, nearly hidden by the plumbing. She carefully knelt down and read it: ARCS ARE FAILED CIRCLES.

Emerging from the restroom, she ran into a blaze of color. It was Duke.

"Thanks for pretending to know me," she said.

"I wasn't pretending."

She waited.

"Amazing what a change in styling and color will do. A different application of makeup. It transforms the features, puts them just enough out of kilter that you're suddenly unrecognizable – to the untrained eye."

"You seem to know a lot about makeup, Duke," she said. "You a tranny?"

"I've got my disguises, Gloria, but that's not one of them. You're Gloria Whiting, aren't you."

She bit her lip.

"I've seen your photo around. Not the cover of *Rolling Stone*, but you're getting some notice. Multimedia performance artist, right? You do it all. Paint, write, act, dance. You were in the papers a couple weeks ago. Something about going into the hospital. Nothing serious, I hope."

"You've got me mixed up with someone else."

He shrugged, sipped his drink. "Okay, suppose you're not who I think. Still, I'm curious what you're doing here."

"One has to be somewhere. That seems to be an underlying principle of existence."

"You don't belong here," he said, growing impatient.

"And you do? What makes you so sure this isn't my world?"

He looked her up and down. "Gloria, take a hint. This isn't the night to be at Ja Ja's."

She studied him a moment, beginning to understand. "Maybe I'm a cop, too."

He looked quickly about and gave her a harsh look. "You're not, that's for sure." He hesitated. "You *are* Gloria Whiting, aren't you?"

"You persist in being mistaken." She turned to leave.

"Listen. I'm sorry. I guess I mixed you up with someone else. You seem like a nice person, and – well, I just don't want you getting unwanted publicity."

"I'll take my chances." She started past, only to be blocked by his arm.

"One last bit of advice. That Shakes over there. He's not exactly Mister Nice Guy. He goes off at regular intervals. And he's due. If I were you, I'd stay clear of him."

"What did he do? Kill his wife or something?"

He gaped at her. "You know?"

She started to walk off again, but then came back. "What do you know about the Rainbow Killer?"

He snorted. "You heard it from the others. He's a huge man with an axe who's killed dozens of people in the Houston slums."

"And you believe that?"

He sighed. "Last November a guy named Harry Cole killed three people in the Bottoms. He tried to beat the rap by blaming someone else – a big man with an axe who was singing Dorothy's song. That's who made him do it. Since then, every killer's been using him as a scapegoat. Sure, the Rainbow Killer made 'em do it."

"What about the witnesses? Hasn't there been quite a few?"

"You bet. Only when you start asking them questions, they don't agree on anything – except the one thing: the song. They all heard a man singing 'Over the Rainbow.' Well, hello-o. Ever since Harry Cole's story hit the papers, everyone's been singing that goddamned song. Christ, just listen!"

A half-dozen people still sang it.

"But how do you explain the clustering? You know, several murders occurring at the same place and time."

Duke gave a smug grin. "Back in high school I saw this corny film that explained fission. You know, how the atom bomb works. They had this roomful of mousetraps all with Ping-Pong balls in them. You set one off, and it sets off others, and pretty soon they're all going off. That's the slums. Too many fuckups with too many guns living too close together. It sure doesn't take a Rainbow Killer to set them off." He paused. "Why are you so interested in him?"

"I'd like to get home alive tonight," she said. "People keep telling me it's not safe."

"I'll take you home."

"I'm in capable enough hands – " she nodded towards Shakes " – as long as there's no Rainbow Killer out there waiting for me."

"In that case, maybe I'm wrong and he does exist."

"Now you're patronizing me." Again she started to leave.

"So how about we get together some other time?" he pressed. "Some-where classier."

"Classier?"

"Dinner at Adagios? Tomorrow night at eight?"

She studied his handsome face. "I'll think about it."

"How do I get in touch with you?"

"You don't. I'll either show, or I won't."

She returned to Shakes's side to find him nursing another beer.

"Long talk," he said. "How's it going with Mister Soul Train?"

"He's a cop," she said.

Shakes sat up straight. "What did you say?"

"He's a cop," she repeated, louder.

Shakes and others close by looked over at Duke. Whispers quickly spread. The room grew silent, except for the rap music in the background. Duke looked very self-conscious as everyone stared at him.

"Shit," he said, starting for the door. "Shit!"

Ja Ja emerged from the back room in a huff, having been told. "Out!" he shouted, even as everyone marched for the door. "All of you, out of my fucking life! Christ! Fuckin' cops everywhere!"

Just outside, Gloria and Shakes ran into Honker.

"Shakes," he said. "Get rid of her. She's trouble for everyone she meets."

"Come on, Honker," he said. "She helped us out, don't you see?"

"She don't read right, Shakes. She don't read right at all."

"Yeah? Well, maybe it's time I got literate. So lay off."

Honker left, cursing aloud.

Gloria had drunk three beers, and her walk was unsteady as they headed back to the hotel. By her count, Shakes had downed six. He ranted about Duke being a cop, and what he'd do to him if they crossed paths again.

"You weren't kidding about killing your wife," she said as they walked down the street.

"Heck no," he said. "I did her in. Just like I told you."

"You're okay now?"

"I was always okay. See, the way people behave, it's like rolling dice. You roll dice long enough, sooner or later you come up homicide. Doesn't mean anything's wrong with you." He made a gesture of dismissal. "Just a roll of the dice."

Gloria noticed that a car was following them, keeping its distance, its lights off.

"Have you seen him?" she asked.

"Who?"

"The Rainbow Killer."

"Yeah, sure, talk to him every day. Know what he told me? He don't exist."

A moment later he added, "I killed my wife all on my own. I mean, there wasn't no 'Over the Rainbow' playing in my head. Same with all those other motherfuckers. They just wants a scapegoat. Fucking cowards. You do something, you take responsibility. Know what I mean?"

She dropped her purse and stooped to pick it up, stealing a glance behind. The car kept its distance. "So you live in a tenement?"

"A dump. A real dump."

"I want to see it."

"No!" He walked faster. "You're crazy."

"Come on, Shakes. I saw some more graffiti."

He stopped and turned to her. "Fluorescent Orange?"

She nodded. "Show me your place. Then I'll tell you what it said."

"Shit." He dug his hands deep in his pockets, then started to walk. "You don't play fair, you know that?"

In a large dilapidated tenement building, six stories up, he kicked hallway debris aside and opened a battered, numberless door. Several notes lay on the floor just inside. She recognized some as rent notices.

"You haven't been home in a while," she said.

"Been on vacation," he grumbled.

Stepping inside, she looked around. Clothes were scattered everywhere, mixed with newspapers, empty food containers and porn magazines. Gnats churned the air, and several roaches fled before her. Graffiti covered the walls, all done in fluorescent orange. She studied it.

"You want something to drink?"

"A glass of water is all." She stepped closer to the wall. "Shakes. This guy you're looking for. You sure it isn't you?"

"Naw." He brought her the glass of water and then busied himself straightening up. "That stuff was just practice. I thought maybe if I could think like him, I could find him." He tossed pornzines under the bed. "Only it's not that easy, I guess. You said you found more o' his graffiti?"

"An arc is a failed circle."

He repeated it several times to himself. "What the fuck? What's he trying to say? Shit, he's so deep sometimes."

Everywhere she looked, she saw pornzines. She walked over and sat down on the bed.

Shakes fidgeted and started mumbling to himself.

"Something wrong, Shakes?"

He dipped deeper than usual across the room, waving his hands. "Why're you here with me? Duke, he's the one for you. But you squealed on him. I mean, this is fuckin' crazy."

"You really wanted me to go with him?" she asked. "Are you that afraid of him?"

"Shee-it. I ain't afraid o' that muthafucka. I shoulda bopped him good back there. A goddamned cop. Pretendin' to be one of us. He better never ever show his face again."

Getting up, she strolled over to the open window and leaned back against the sill. In between sips of water she let loose with a bloodcurdling scream, being very nonchalant about it.

Shakes stared wide-eyed at her, completely flabbergasted. A car door slammed. The tenement door squeaked open below, and footsteps clanged up the stairs. Soon there was pounding on the door.

"Open up, Shakes! I'm counting to three. One. Two."

Having sauntered over to the door, Gloria now unlocked it. Duke barged in with gun leveled at Shakes, who stood in the corner with hands up and eyes wide.

"You okay, Gloria?"

"I'm fine," she said. "And you?"

He looked at her uncomprehendingly. "I – I heard someone scream. I thought it was you." He began to look apologetic.

"It was."

He was at a loss. "Why did you scream?"

"I just had the urge. Something primeval, I guess."

Furious and bewildered, he lowered his gun, then backstepped to the door. There he hesitated, glaring at her. "Lady." His voice quavered. "You've got one lousy sense of humor."

He slammed the door so hard that she jumped involuntarily. She listened to his rapid footfalls, the pinging on the staircase, the slam of the tenement door below. A car door opened and shut, an engine roared to life, and tires squealed time and again as he raced off into the city.

"You could've got me killed!" Shakes cried. "You – !"

She went over and lay down on the bed. "So. Who are you more afraid of? Duke? The Rainbow Killer?" She gave him a provocative look. "Or me?"

He just stood there with his mouth agape.

"Well? Which is it?"

"Christ, you're fucking with my mind. You're really fucking with my mind!" He paced back and forth, clawing the air to either side of his face. "Why don't you leave me alone?"

"I've got business with the Rainbow Killer. Something tells me this might be the place to find him."

In a softer but still irritated voice, punctuated by hard breathing, he said, "Shit. Why you keep fuckin' with my head? Why you wanna do that?" He ran his hands through his hair. "I gotta think. I gotta – " He turned to her. "You a cop? Is that it? You a cop too?"

"What makes you think that?"

"All these questions about the Rainbow Killer. You working with Duke? The pair of you double-pumping me? You think I'm him?"

"No, Shakes. I'm not a cop."

He stood there, looking dizzy. "Then what the fuck are you?" He gripped his head. "I – I gotta get out. I can't stay here."

"Go on. I'll watch the place for you."

He looked back at her. "Hey, no. No. You can't be here alone. I got friends might drop in. Sort of friends. You don't wanna be here if they do."

"But they won't drop in, will they," she said. "Because they're just as afraid of the Rainbow Killer."

He tossed pornzines across the room. "I'm not afraid of no fucking Rainbow Killer!"

Lying on the bed, watching Shakes pace back and forth, she realized she was getting sleepy. "You *do* believe in him, don't you," she murmured.

He ducked his head in exaggerated nods. "He's out there. He. Is. Out. There."

"Why do you suppose he sings 'Over the Rainbow'?"

"Why does he – ? Yeah, yeah. He wants to change the world, I suppose. Make it a better place." He slowed to a stop in front of the window. "A better place. Yeah, what's the word?"

"Utopia?"

"That's it. That's what he wants. He sings 'Over the Rainbow' 'cause over there it's a better world." He leaned out the window and took a deep breath of the night. "Yeah, utopia." He turned to her, settling back on the sill. "He goes in ghettos, brings out the deep, dark shit in lowlifes, triggers 'em like a gun, so they go off, make a big killing spree, and right in front of the cops so they get fingered good, put 'em away permanent. That's his agenda, his road to utopia. And he's due. He is so fucking due."

She watched him try to sit still on the sill, but he kept rocking and dipping. "Shakes? Does the name Gloria Whiting mean anything to you?"

"Nope. Maybe I heard it, but I don't know."

"Well, that's me. That's who I am. I've been in some art mags, had a performance on PBS. I'm a multimedia performance artist."

He looked at her, not really comprehending.

"Let me tell you what I do. It's all very spontaneous. There's no script. I paint, sculpt, dance; I compose music and I sing. I do stuff like that and more, all mixed together. And I record it all, the whole process, the whole ordeal. That's what it is: an ordeal. Because there's something in me that's trying to get out. That's what my art's all about, trying to express what's in me. I work nonstop for days, not eating, not sleeping, and I can feel it. I feel myself getting close to what's inside – something huge, full of significance, a great truth. But I never reach it. I always collapse before I get there. I just don't have the stamina, the strength..."

She caught herself and gave a nervous laugh. "How melodramatic I must sound – ridiculous, even. Still, my doctors, they tell me this has to stop. I'm destroying my health. For years I've ignored them, but I can't anymore. Because they're right; it gets harder. It gets harder every time."

A siren wailed in the distance, setting off a chorus of barks.

"Does any of this make sense, Shakes? What I'm saying?"

He stared at the fluorescent orange scrawls on the wall. "So you come here hopin' to meet Mister Rainbow Killer. You want him to help you bring it out, so you can see."

She nodded. "Which is totally crazy. Because, first off, he probably doesn't exist. And if he does, I'd be meeting him on his terms, in the middle of murder and mayhem, my life on the line. But I don't care. I no longer care. I'm willing to risk all just to know. I have to know what's inside me."

She took several slow, deep breaths, calming herself. "You ever feel that way?"

He shook his head like a top out of control. "I know what's in me. Bad stuff, 'cause I wasn't raised right. I done bad stuff and I'll do it again. It's best not to stir me up, you know? If there's something important floating around, it's not in me. It's out there. Maybe there." His finger shook as he pointed at the wall. "Fluorescent Orange knows something important, and I'm trying to figure it out. That's my head-game, I guess. But sometimes I just look at his stuff and think, 'This guy don't know shit.'"

She laughed softly, thinking about it. Watching the play of light and shadow around him as he rocked, she felt herself drifting towards sleep. The siren faded and the dogs stopped barking. Then the door on the ground floor creaked open and clanged shut. Shakes stopped rocking and strained his ears. Gloria listened too. She heard the faintest voice. Deep and melodious, it echoed through the building's interior.

"It's Duke," she said, seeing Shakes tense up.

"But he drove off!"

"He stopped a couple blocks away and walked back. It's Duke."

Shakes remained unconvinced.

"It took him a while," she continued, "but he finally figured out a way to get even – or try to." She smiled at him. "Come on, Shakes. Don't let him spook you."

Shakes had begun to hyperventilate.

"Come on, Shakes."

A scream pierced the night, coming from somewhere below. Gloria sat up, chilled. Shakes jumped forward and fumbled a gun from under the mattress. In seconds he was at the door, standing next to it, his back to the wall. His lips were rounded, puffing hard and fast, sweat beading on his forehead.

"It's just someone else panicking," Gloria said, trying to convince herself as well. She sought the pulse of her subconscious, checking for something rising up, preparing to emerge. But all she got was her own rattled nerves. Shakes's gun worried her most.

"Come on, Shakes," she said, standing up. "Give me the gun."

"No!" His breathing was ragged. "Shit no! That's him!" He gasped. "And he's coming up here. I can feel it."

"I tell you, it's Duke. Let's at least call the police. They'll handle it. Where's your phone?"

"What fucking phone! You think I got a fucking phone?"

The singing grew louder and more off-key. There was now no doubting the song. A commotion came from below, followed by muffled cries.

"Oh shit! He's coming!" Shakes wailed, shifting his weight foot to foot.

"We're fine, Shakes." She walked slowly toward him. "He won't hurt us."

"You think I'm scared of him? Shit! It's what's in here!" He palmed the side of his head.

She looked from him to the gun in his hand. They shook out of sync. "You've got a good soul, Shakes. I can tell. Now give me the gun."

"Bullshit! I got anger. I got hatred. Oh, shit, I'm fucked!"

"Then the gun won't do you any good, Shakes," she said, fighting down her own panic. "Give it to me."

"Give it to you!" he shrieked. "Christ, you're fucking crazier than I ever was." He tried to laugh, but it came out as sharp raspy breaths.

Gloria stopped. The gun was pointed her way. "Fine, Shakes. Throw it out the window. Just get rid of it."

Eyes wild, he shook his head. "He's got an axe, 'member? I ain't facing no axe unarmed!"

She felt her terror rising as he took more ragged breaths. Footfalls clanged on the stairs, the voice growing louder and clearer. She kept waiting for the clank of an access door opening onto another floor, but it never came. His footfalls continued up the metal steps, ever closer. Time seemed to stand still. Then an access door creaked open. Soon after, it clanked shut. The deep voice resumed, off-key, echoing through the corridor just outside.

"Shakes," she said.

As the footsteps grew steadily louder, Shakes's gun hand quavered uncontrollably.

"Shakes, no."

"Bitch! Fuckin' white bitch!" he slurred. He swung the gun upward, slamming the butt end against his temple. He struck himself twice, hard. She winced at the ghastly *klok! klok!*.

Then his hand was on the doorknob.

"Shakes?"

"Muthafuck!" he shouted, blood dribbling down the side of his head. "Muthafuck!" He wrenched the door open and plunged into the hallway. The door rebounded and closed.

Gloria jumped at each gunshot. There were five of them in rapid succession, then one more. She pressed against the door, listening for some sound.

"Shakes?" she whispered. "Shakes!"

The footsteps resumed, slow and steady, drawing closer, as did the deep, off-key singing. She fumbled with the door lock, at last getting it latched, then braced herself against the door. She felt something massive coming down the hallway, axe in hand, dripping blood.

The footsteps stopped just outside the door, as did the singing. She stepped back, heart pounding, as the knob turned one way, then the other. At any moment she expected an axe to splinter the door. Nothing happened. She stared at the door. Then came a soft chuckle. It wasn't Shakes.

"What have we here? Nobody home?"

The voice was deep, delivering another chuckle; and now she felt something astir deep within. She sank to the floor as he continued, more in her head than aloud: "So many artists, so little message. Some have nothing to say, and it's their fear of the inner void that makes them create so much."

A deep rumble of laughter filled the corridor even as that monstrous inner thing breached upon her consciousness, a vast emptiness that dissipated into the night without a trace.

The footsteps resumed soon after that, slow, in retreat, accompanied by the singing; and with it came shrieks and something slamming into a wall, followed by a man's loud bellow and muffled gunshots.

Minutes later, with police sirens wailing, she recovered her wits enough to open the door. Shakes sat propped against the wall, blood caking the side of his head and soaking his shirt. He appeared semiconscious. The gun lay at his side.

"Shakes?"

He shuddered and blinked. Then he looked up at her. "I missed. Six shots, and I fucking missed." Almost as an afterthought he laughed.

The sirens grew louder, and the wall in Shakes's room reflected a flashing red.

"You okay, Shakes?"

Looking down at his bloodied shirt, he gave a tired smile and began to dip. "Yeah. Yeah, I think I am. Biggest muthafucka I ever saw, and he walked straight through me."

She reached down and gingerly picked up his gun. It was still warm from firing. Using a corner of her dress, she gave it a thorough wipe-off; then, gripping it through the fabric of her dress, she flung it as far as she could down the hallway.

"He was big," Shakes said, twisting up his face, trying to remember. "Maybe he didn't go through me, but he got by. He got to you, to the door, was trying to get in. He was after you, Princess."

She checked his temple. It was swollen and still bleeding. "No, Shakes.

I don't think so." She ripped a piece of hem from her dress. "I don't think he had any use for me at all."

"Well, that's good then. That's good. I'm glad. But – ? How 'bout you? You use him? You make him show you what's inside?"

Settling down beside him, she pressed the cloth against his temple. "I suppose I did." She felt dizzy, disoriented. The foggy road ahead had entirely vanished. She had no idea where she was headed anymore. "It wasn't pretty, Shakes. Not pretty at all."

"Yeah? So you got some evil stuff in you?"

Sitting there, she felt like she might never get up again. "No, Shakes. I'm afraid not."

STEALING FROM GARBO

RON SAVAGE

If you had his trust, he would tell you what thrills him. To take what is yours and make it mine, he would say. Then he'd say, There's nothing better. He compares it to sex or a T-bone medium rare. He likes to say, It's better than sipping a cold Corona with lime on a Jamaican beach. Or the Mets winning the pennant. He would tell you the one thing all thieves know. Stealing is the drug of choice.

It's 1976, Cincinnati has taken the series from the Yankees. *One Flew Over the Cuckoo's Nest* wins Best Picture, and The Captain and Tennille are singing 'Love Will Keep Us Together (Forever)'. His wife has left him. Don't even think about looking for me, this is what her note reads. He finds it on the gray Formica table in the kitchen. Bobbi J has taken the twins, his boys. She has taken everything but the water bed and the kitchen things. His house is as empty as he feels. A glittering two inches of jewelry covers the black and white tile floor of the bathroom. There are gold brooches and Cartier and Rolex watches. There are necklaces and bracelets studded with diamonds and sapphires and rubies. Another note is taped to the bathroom mirror. This one reads, You said you weren't doing this anymore, Nicholas. Now I am stealing us away from you. How do you like it? Bobbi J. She always knew what button to press and for how long. This time 'long' might be very long. Nicholas doesn't like it.

The Campanile is a fourteen story brown brick co-op on East 52nd

Street. It was built in the thirties, an uncluttered, stoic-looking building that is at the end of a dead end street and overlooks the east river. There is no canopy or roof deck or garage or sidewalk landscaping. There are no balconies. It has sixteen apartments, a pool, and a doorman named Derek.

Nicholas has become friends with the doorman and knows what Derek does and doesn't like. He is a vegetarian. He has a Pekinese named Charlie. Derek was also married for fifty-three years and is a recent widower. When Derek and Charlie can't sleep, which is most of the time, they watch old movies together in Derek's brown leather recliner. They are great Paul Newman fans. Derek's favorites are *The Drowning Pool, Cool Hand Luke,* and *Harper.* Charlie likes Paul's lighter films, *Butch Cassidy and the Sundance Kid,* for example, and *Rally 'Round the Flag, Boys!.* Nicholas has been reading up on Paul Newman and vegetarianism and Pekinese dogs. Derek thinks Nicholas is Bill Kramer, Jr who owns a plumbing business on West 55th. Sometimes Derek and Nicholas go out for drinks after Derek finishes his doorman duties. They talk about easy to do vegetarian recipes. Mostly, though, they talk about Paul Newman and what Paul is doing now and how wonderful it is that Paul and his lovely wife Joanne Woodward have stayed married. Derek has even promised Bill to send some Campanile business his way.

That's not necessary, Nicholas/Bill says.

What are friends for? Derek says.

Nicholas understands why Bobbi J was so quick to leave. But he's been a good provider for her and the boys and has never cheated. Bobbi is a large girl with a pretty face and tiny feet. Nick's sister, Anita, introduced them six years ago.

You'll like her, Anita had said to Nicholas. Anita has intense gray eyes that take you in and never blink. His sister said, You like blondes, right? Who doesn't. She has a great personality and a really pretty face.

So she's fat, Nicholas said.

She was fat, absolutely fat, not big-boned, not a couple pounds over. Bobbi J was short and round, five-three, two-eleven, and it just didn't matter. There are people you feel at home with from the start. Like a key finding its lock, you hear the click and feel the tumbling bolts through your fingertips. Nicholas feels that way; he thought she felt that way, too.

Bobbi J never asked Nicholas how he earned his money, another reason he liked her. When you meet the right woman, you know. He gave her a five carat Asscher cut engagement ring. He built her a beautiful two story Victorian with a heart shaped pool in upscale Clinton, thirty miles north of Trenton. On their first anniversary Bobbi J opened the front door and found a silver Mercedes 280SE tied with a red ribbon in the driveway. Nicholas wanted to show his love. Nicholas wanted a wife who was an accomplice.

You spoil me, Bobbi J said.

That's my joy, Nicholas said.

The twins changed Bobbi J more than Nicholas, though both agreed the changes were for the better. The first time Nicholas saw the twins he thought, You're daddy's boys. Ernest and Eric. They already had his dark hair and thick eyelashes and beautiful Greek skin. They were slim and graceful like him. They also had small hands with long fingers. Those hands got everyone's attention from the start. Bobbi J's granny said it best. Granny Lott is short like Bobbi J but she has lavender eyes and not an ounce of fat anywhere. After studying the boys in their Graco Duorider stroller, she said, They have the hands of thieves.

The woman who lives on the fifth floor of the Campanile keeps to her schedule. Nicholas has been writing down her times and places in a pocket-sized spiral notebook. Derek the doorman says the woman keeps her phone in the lobby. It's got the letter G on it. The phone rings but it's never answered. Derek says she is up at 7:00am to cook her own breakfast before the maid arrives.

Nicholas enjoys following Ms G. She wears large shady hats and Jackie O sunglasses. The sunglasses hide everything but her nose, lips, and chin. He enjoys the preciseness of her life, the on-time routine of it. Ms G is like a German train, she is tidy and never late. She leaves at 9:00am and returns at 12:30 for lunch. Not 12:31, not 12:29. Ms G walks the quieter, less traveled streets. Her favorites are First and Second avenues. And the day doesn't end here. Derek says she eats her lunch at 1:00pm, usually tuna or chicken salad, sometimes just fruit. A new trip into town begins at 1:30pm. The afternoons are devoted to art galleries, especially the ones on Madison Avenue.

Nicholas has begun looking forward to the gallery visits. He'd always thought art was for people who wore black clothes and handmade jewelry but now finds he like the surrealists. Yesterday Nicholas followed Ms G into the La Fiandra Gallery on Madison and 73rd. The gallery has a bleached pine floor and white walls and angled lighting. He was examining a Chagall when he felt the woman staring at him from behind her Jackie O's, from beneath the shadowy wide-brim hat. Nicholas turned and glanced at her, less than a second, nothing obvious. She was on the opposite side of the narrow room. And wasn't that a smile?

The two men had walked into Bobbi J's home without asking. This was five or six months ago, more like six. They didn't talk or give her a nod or notice her. The twins were playing with Lego in the living room. Ernest was building a square of alternating red and black rows, and Eric was throwing the loose red ones at Ernest. The two men were tall and big-shouldered and wore dark suits with white shirts and ties and gold cufflinks. One had a droopy brown mustache and the other was clean-shaven and smoked a cigar. They looked in all the upstairs and downstairs rooms. Then the one with the mustache told the twins to shut the fuck up. When Bobbi J said, Hey, you, wait just a minute, the man with the cigar slapped her across the face and sent her to the floor. Ernest and Eric started crying. The two men ignored them. The clean-shaven one with the cigar knelt on one knee and fastened his thick fingers around Bobbi J's throat.

Where's your husband? he said. His voice was calm, close to bored, the way people get after doing the same job for awhile.

I don't ask him, Bobbi J said. She was having trouble breathing.

A peacekeeper, the man with the cigar said. Then he said, Okay, peacekeeper, tell hubby we want our business concluded by nine. He's two days late. If we don't get what's ours by nine, we'll see you and the kids at nine-thirty.

Nicholas was home an hour later and Bobbi J started throwing dishes at him and screaming. The twins were upstairs in the bed, still fussy and sobbing. Now they were calling for Bobbi J.

I must be crazy, Bobbi J said. She knew Ernest and Eric were crying but couldn't stop herself to comfort them. She was too angry, too frightened. Bobbi J felt she was speeding down a hill and couldn't find the brake. She said, It's like I'm a drug addict. I got the beautiful home with the pool. I got the fancy-shmancy car. I got enough fur in my closet to start a zoo. And I forget. No, no, not forget. I ignore, okay? I sweep what you do under a rug.

Hey, c'mon, relax, Nicholas said. His left arm was angled sideways in front of his face to bat away the in-coming dishes. He ducked and batted, ducked and batted. Dishes were shattering all around him. Nicholas was saying, Can you relax? Can you do that? C'mon, Bobbi, honey. Can you relax for a minute?

Bobbi J hadn't quit screaming. She said, I tell myself it's government work. My husband, the spy. I actually think that. That's how crazy I am. That's how much I want my house and my things. She said, But you're not a spy. You're nothing, Nicky. You're a thief. You're a stupid, stupid thief.

He managed to get her quiet, Nicholas the therapist. He was sitting spread-legged behind her, his arms wrapped about hers to keep her from slapping him or throwing more dishes.

Okay, shhh, shhh, Nicholas whispered. Bobbi J had started to cry. Between her and the kids, it was a real cry fest. She told him about the man with the mustache and the man with the cigar. Nicholas said, That's done. I forgot to do what I needed to do, that's all.

We have the boys now, Bobbi J said.

I'll get a real job, Nicholas said. He cocked his head down and kissed her cheek. He said, You know I love you. Things'll be different.

Promise me, Bobbi J said and sniffed.

Sure, absolutely, he said.

Nicholas has just walked into Ms G's apartment. He wears his white jumpsuit. FIFTY-FIFTH STREET PLUMBING is stenciled on the back in black gothic letters. He has done his research on Ms G and feels confident. Nicholas will tell you there are four types of thieves, the Opportunist, the Smasher, the Prowler, and the Pro. He considers himself a Pro. A Pro can be either a Sniper or a Locust. The Sniper goes after one item. The Locust cleans out the house. Nicholas has done both and prefers Sniper work. Tonight, though, he is a Locust but a Locust who won't get greedy. Two or three items only, and he prefers jewelry.

His timing must be just so, timing is everything. The maid leaves at four-thirty; Ms G arrives at five-thirty. It's a forty minute window, if he wants a cushion.

The entry has been easy. Nicholas isn't a Smasher, Nicholas doesn't force doors or use crowbars or break locks. He is a class act. Take this morning, for example. Derek the doorman calls Nicholas and tells him an attorney on the third floor needs a garbage disposal installed. The job comes with Derek's pass key. Did he steal from the lawyer? No, Nicholas isn't an Opportunist, either. Just because it's there to steal doesn't mean you steal it. The installation took twenty minutes and the elevator ride from the third floor to Ms G's on the fifth floor took three minutes.

Four of the rooms in her apartment are bedrooms. Along with these are a dining room, a kitchen, a walk-in pantry, a laundry room, staff quarters, and more bathrooms than anyone would ever need. A yellow, rose, and white oriental rug covers most of the polished dark wood floor of the living room. The ceiling, the mantel, and the lacquered walls are all subdued yellow. Above the fireplace is a painting of a mother and child. Nicholas doesn't recognize them. Two ornate red velvet chairs are on either side of the fireplace. The wall behind the chairs has built-in shelves filled with books, their bindings arranged in groups of umber and yellow. It's a warm but formal room, tasteful but obsessive, not unlike the owner.

Men used to follow me because they wanted sex, she says. Now they just want my money.

She poses at the archway of the foyer, leaning against it, arms folded to her chest, looking into the living room. The woman is wearing baggy gray silk pants, white and gray loafers, and a white silk blouse. She's seventy-one now, still tall, slim, her hair shoulder-length and straight.

You've been following me for awhile, she says. It's a European accent, though nothing Nicholas can attach to a country. She says, But today I don't see you at all. And I think to myself, the day's not over.

As the woman enters the living room, more like drifting into it, she is unhooking a diamond bracelet and gold watch from her left wrist. She tosses them to Nicholas while lowering herself into one of the red velvet chairs and crossing her legs at the knee. From the foyer to the chair is a singular fluid motion.

You haven't called the police, Nicholas says. It's a statement.

The night's early, she says.

Nicholas figures he is holding seventy-five thousand dollars worth of jewelry, not that he'd get that much. He might end up with thirty, maybe thirty-five. Selling someone else's jewelry is expensive.

I adore thieves, Ms G says. She glances down at her long thin fingers. The nails are manicured and dark red. She says, The movie business is full of thieves. They used to call me a thief, you know. If a woman negotiates well, movie people think she's either a thief or a lesbian. If you do it very well, they think you're both.

Nicholas slips the diamond bracelet and the gold watch into the breast pocket of his jumpsuit. His stomach has started tightening. This happens when he feels uneasy. He isn't sure where her talk is going. Maybe she's lonely or only being friendly. Maybe she has already called the police. How do you tell? She is still an actress.

I'll leave you alone, Nicholas says.

I never said that, she says. 'I *vont* to be alone.' Isn't that how it's done? Like I'm a vaudeville comedian. What I said was, 'I want to be left alone.' But only by people who bore me.

I didn't mean it that way, Nicholas says. I just have to go.

Stealing from a willing mark is unnerving enough without having to chat with the person. Nicholas feels like a hooker who has to listen to a john after sex. Free talk is bad business. His stomach won't quit bothering him.

I thought we might exchange stories, she says. One thief to another.

You think you're like me? Nicholas says. He can't believe this shit. He tells her, I lost my family. I lost everything.

I think we're both negotiators, she says and rubs away something from the white top of her gray and white shoe. Do you know what makes a good negotiator?

Nicholas is driving back to Jersey in his rented white Chevy Econoline. He's tired and doesn't want to think about what makes a good negotiator. Ms G is lonely, that's all, too lonely and too old. The conversation had droned on forever. Her monologue. All she wanted was him as an audience; he'd barely listened to the woman.

Nicholas thinks he should drive to Trenton and see if Bobbi J and the twins are staying with Bobbi J's mother and crazy Granny Lott. Even if Bobbi J isn't there, maybe one of them knows something. He takes exit 7A toward Trenton. Headlights glide around him. They flash his rearview mirror like bright silent explosions. Nicholas wants to tell Bobbi J the truth. He wants to tell her that she is his wife and he loves her but stealing is an old girlfriend who calls him up at three in the morning and talks dirty.

A good negotiator is possessed. Ms G says this in a European accent that has lost its origin. She is seated on one of the two red velvet chairs that frame the fireplace, her legs crossed at the knee. Tonight Ms G is dressed in a white silk blouse and gray silk slacks and gray and white shoes. Seventy-one years old and Nicholas can still see her beauty. He also has seen her movies and knows what the camera saw in the 1920s and the 1930s. Then she says to him, We will give up everything for the deal. Isn't that what a good negotiator is willing to do? We will walk away from all of it.

Nicholas says nothing. He takes the diamond bracelet and the gold watch from the breast pocket of his jumpsuit and lays the jewelry on the red velvet ottoman next to Ms G. He is thinking how selling someone else's jewelry is expensive. He is thinking of the quieter, less traveled streets and the empty galleries.   ⚄

DOGWOOD

SUSAN OVERCASH WALKER

The wreckers squatted in the dirt, in the space between the tow trucks, flipping a coin to see who would pull my submerged Buick out of the Everson town lake. There were three truckers in the tri-county area that had crane and wrench equipment capable of traversing the fifty feet of water to where the car had fetched up, after I'd driven it off a boat dock with seventeen-year-old Lily Trevino shivering in the passenger seat. I had held her, her small body jerking against me, as the brackish water rose up over the hood and the windows. It was a lot like watching an aquarium fill up from the inside, I'd decided, just before the door seals completely eroded and the pressure reached maximum force, busting the windows and sending a tidal wave of water and glass into the front seat. She was gone now, but I was still here, perched in a dogwood tree along the edge of the lake, watching the action and chattering like a monkey with the blue jays and mockingbirds on the branches.

It had taken the sheriff and Lily's parents a week to figure out what happened. At first the cops thought Lily had taken off to New York or LA; by the time they found her car abandoned out on Route 751, we were both dead. The sheriff put out an Amber Alert, sent her picture to all the network stations and organized a search operation in the woods with the volunteer community watch group. They didn't get it, though, the sheriff or the state troopers or the neighbors or her parents, until the groundskeeper at the summer house I'd been camping at finally found the duct tape and the tire tracks and Lily's high-heel sandal near the boat house. After that, it didn't take long for Sheriff Benton to get the idea. I was sitting on the Trevinos' counter when the sheriff broke the news that they might have a lead on where she was – not where she was, but where her body was – and that they were calling in the state divers for assistance. Her mother had screamed and fallen onto the linoleum floor. Her father had cried.

A wrecker in a stained work shirt won the toss. He shook hands with the other two and walked over to the sheriff and the two divers standing on the boat dock, staring into the sullen brown water.

"Ready?" he asked. The sheriff nodded.

"Damn shame," one of the divers said, shaking his head. "It's a damn shame."

The divers had found the Buick earlier in the morning, a breezy Thursday morning in early March, with the dogwoods blooming and nodding like oversized cotton balls from the lake front. Sheriff Benton had called them in from the state on Tuesday, but it took a day or two to round up the appropriate personnel, and hell, it was pretty straightforward that she was dead as soon as the sheriff put two-and-two together. If I could get any of them to see or hear me I might even tell them about it myself, about how she had cried when I held her down and then after I was through with her, tied her hands and took the duct tape off her mouth. None of the town folk could hear her yelling as far out across the lake as we were, and March in the Carolinas was still too chilly for any of the summer folk to have made it back up yet. It was just her and me and the Buick and the night.

The funny thing was, she hadn't screamed when I took the tape off her mouth. She cried and whimpered at first, but then she just stared at me, the whites of her eyes swallowing the black of her pupils. I tied her up against a tree trunk and pulled out a pack of cigarettes, thinking about the cold feeling of the water rushing up over us. We were fifty feet from the dock, back behind the boat house underneath a couple of the dogwood trees. The light from the Buick's open trunk cast a mellow glow across her skinny frame.

"What now?" she asked finally, her hands twisting against the nylon rope behind her. She was trying to untie herself, but it was useless; too many years of practice had taught me the rights and wrongs of tying a woman up. Above us, the moon cast silver hieroglyphs on the lake beyond the boat dock.

I shrugged. "We'll see," I told her, and grinned a little. Her bone-white forehead glistened. "You can stop now," I told her, nodding at her wriggling. "You can't untie it. I made sure."

Her pupils dilated for a moment, and her back stiffened. Her skirt was still all screwed up around her waist, and she twisted her legs away from me in a shallow attempt at modesty. She had kicked off one of her shoes in the struggle. Had it been a different day, I would have made sure the shoe and the duct tape all got put away, in the wheel well of the car or maybe down into the lake with her. But it was a special day for both of us.

"So what, then?" she asked. "You're going to kill me?"

I pulled my second-to-last cigarette out of the pack and lit it, inhaling deeply. "Wouldn't be the first time," I told her, blowing smoke into the breeze. The trees rustled above us, a few white blossoms from the dogwoods drifting down onto my shoulders.

She stared at me, stopping the struggling. She was a marble statue, sitting there in the moonlight, all pale skin and ash blonde hair. She might have made it in LA or New York, if not for me. It was heady stuff, the power I had over her. I could kill her at any time. I could make her scream again. But then that voice, that goddamn voice in my head started up again: *wrongwrongwrongbadwrong.* I ashed my cigarette and stood up, walked over to the Buick and leaned up against the bumper.

"You're going to kill me," she said, tilting her head back against the tree.

"Why's that?"

"Because I'm looking at you. You would hide your face otherwise."

I shrugged. "Maybe," I told her. "It's a good point." I took another puff of my cigarette. Nut-grass tufted up through the hard-packed dirt at my feet.

"Who are you?" she asked. "You should at least tell me that." I could see all the bad murder-mysteries she had ever read crawl across her face. "I'm Lily," she said.

I smiled. "Yes, you are," I said.

"You know me?" she asked. When I didn't answer, she started again, her voice tinny against the evening breeze. "I have a family, you know. If you know who I am, then you know that," she said. "A brother. My parents. They'll be freaking out when they find out I'm gone. They'll find my car. They're probably looking for me right now."

I smiled wider. "Probably," I said. It had barely been an hour since we had left her car on the side of the road. I reached over and patted her on the head. She twisted away from me, almost falling over in her haste to get away. I pulled my hand back and shoved it in my pocket. *Dirtywrong.* But it felt so good.

"They'll find you, if you kill me," she said. "But you can still let me go. It's not too late. You can let me go and I'll never say anything. Nobody would ever know."

"Oh for God's sake," I said. A red haze was creeping up behind my eyes. The sound of her voice grated on my nerves like a knife being sharpened. Part of me wanted to kill her just to shut her up. "You can quit the bullshit," I said. "You think I don't know what I'm doing is wrong?" Her eyes widened. Behind her, the moon-shadow of the summer house engulfed the yard. It crept toward us, toward the boat house and the dock and the car, as the moon continued to rise. The voices were coming on again, with the wind and the darkness.

"You want to know the kicker?" I asked her. "I know it's wrong. All I ever hear anymore are these voices in my head telling me it's wrong. And what I want is for all the goddamn voices in my head telling me how wrong it is to stop. Can you get that?"

She shook her head, tears gathering in the corners of her eyes. "N-no."

"Then fucking shut up, Lily." I spat her name out. "Okay? Just shut up." She nodded, crying a little. "Okay." I took the last puff of my second-to-last cigarette and dropped it on the ground.

Watching the divers wade into the water with the pulley trailing behind them, I thought about her again – not about how she felt the first time, between my body and the ground – but how she felt in the car, when I had held her before we died. She had been so small, but hard, her body a bundle of muscle and sinew as she tried to buck out of my grip. She had been screaming when we hit the water, her voice echoing in the cavernous front seat of the Buick, but once the water started to rise around us, she had grown quiet, her eyes eating up her pretty face. For a second, she had been still, so still that I thought she might have passed out, and then she bucked once more, harder than before and I almost lost my grasp. She flailed at me, bit my shoulder, screamed again, and it was all I could do to hold on to her as the water rose around us in a blue and black blanket.

Before that, though, God, she had wanted to talk. It took her a few minutes to get her courage back up after I told her to shut up the first time, but she really thought she could talk me out of it. I should have known; when I first saw her at the Shell station out on Route 751, I had to wait a solid five minutes for her to finish chatting with the store clerk before she came back out to her car. I used a bubble light to pull her over a few miles down the road. It was always the most dangerous part. One minute to get her out of her car. One minute to get her in my trunk – that was the worst part, all quick movements with adrenaline pumping, watching for cars or passers-by coming down the road. One minute to put a white plastic bag in her window, to show she had broken down. And then the heady feeling of power, of control, and the whisper of the voices in the background: *badwrong*. But I couldn't stop.

"I thought you were a cop," she said. "Are you a cop?"

I laughed. "No," I said. "I'm not a cop."

She ducked her head, and I thought she was crying again. Her voice came up from under her hair. "I could help you, maybe," she said. "If you hear voices, maybe we could talk about it. Maybe they're there for a reason."

"Oh, for God's sake, who do you think you are?" I asked her. "I saw you at a goddamn gas station. I hadn't even been following you. That's the kicker. That's it. You were in the wrong goddamn place at the wrong goddamn time. You can't talk to me about anything. I don't want to talk about anything. All I want are for the voices in my head to stop. Can you get that? Can you?" I leaned over her, and she shrank away from me, scooching back against the tree trunk. The voices were screaming again, the red haze creeping back up. God, when had this started? I couldn't control it anymore. I pressed a fist against my temple, towering over her in the amber glow of the trunk light. She sagged at my feet like a sack of rotten fruit.

"You can't make a deal with me, do you get that?" I asked. "Do you get it? I would have let you go already if it were coming to that. But you're going to help me instead." I stepped back and took a deep breath, wheezing a little. "You're going to help me do the right thing. That's the kicker, isn't it? It's the wrong thing, but it's the right thing, too."

"What do you mean?" she asked. If the girl could have shrunk into the tree, she would have.

"You're going to help me end all of this," I told her. "I know it's wrong. I know what I've done is wrong. The voices, they're killing me. So you're going to help me end it."

A horizon of hope dawned across her face. "You want me to kill you?" she asked, her voice very small in the shadow of the summer house behind us.

I laughed as if she had told a very excellent joke, and the tension in my back faded a little. I reached for my cigarettes. There was only one left in the pack. "In a manner of speaking," I said. "You're going to help me die." I lit up the cigarette and coughed a little on the first drag. When I exhaled, the red haze had lifted and the voices were quiet. It was just me again, in control of the machine. "One more to go," I said, and smiled.

The sheriff stood on the boat dock, waiting for the divers' signal, checking his watch. The Trevino family wasn't there, just a pack of state troopers and some folks from the medical examiner's office. Below me, a crime scene unit combed the landscape for clues to my identity. They had already found my pack, the hard place on the ground where Lily had been tied up and I'd had my last cigarette. They were lucky; it hadn't rained in a week, and some of the evidence remained for them to find. I didn't care; I hovered in my dogwood, watching. The white blossoms were starting to turn, the tree fading from snowy white into a cacophony of mint and sage, and every so often I would gather up the energy to rustle the leaves and send a few down onto their stooped backs. I didn't know why Lily wasn't here with me, lurking in the trees or behind the boat house. Every once in a while I would see someone else like me, someone who hovered vaguely in the shadows, a man dressed in 60s style fatigues with a bloody hole in his belly, a farmer with half his skull missing. I couldn't tell if they could see me or not. Lily, though – she was nowhere to be found.

She had prayed a little, when it came to the end. She had watched me smoke for the better part of ten minutes without saying a word, and then she had bucked her chin out and said the one thing I never thought she would say.

"I can't kill you."

I coughed on my inhale. The cigarette was three quarters gone, and the moon was almost at its apex. "Excuse me?"

"I can't kill you," she said again.

"Are you out of your fucking mind?" I asked. "In case you've failed to notice, you don't have a choice in the matter."

"If you want to die, that's fine," she said. "But I can't do it. It's not right with the Lord." She sat up straight against the tree trunk, flexing her elbows as much as she could against the nylon rope. She shrugged her shoulders back, her tits pushing out against the knit of her shirt, and then collapsed back into a slump.

"What the hell are you talking about?" My voice was even, but her words had started my stomach rolling, over and over, like a car going over a cliff. Maybe she was bluffing; but when she looked up at me, her face was ashen and tight with strain, tears making dirty tracks down the skin stretched drum-tight over her cheekbones. I didn't believe she was bluffing.

She shrugged and dropped her head. "I know it sounds stupid."

"You're goddamn right it sounds stupid. It sounds ludicrous."

"I know," she said. "But it's not my call. I can't kill you. There are some things that are right and wrong, and if I killed you, it would be just as wrong as – " She stopped.

"What?" I had to catch my breath a little before I took another drag on the cigarette. "What?"

"As this," she said. "As what you're doing to me. And I can't do that. I'll hit you over the head and run away if I can. But I can't shoot you or stab you or any of that."

I leaned back against the car trunk again and stared at her. The breeze had died, and the night air was still. She sat, not moving, her image flickering in the dim light like a projection from a broken television screen, and for a moment, I couldn't tell if she was really there or just a hallucination, an extension of the voices in my head. I sat like that, silent, afraid to move or even breathe, until the breeze picked up again and blew her hair in a halo around her head and I could tell she was real again. I exhaled my last breath of nicotine, relief and anger washing over me, and dropped the stub, grinding it out in the dirt.

"Well, luckily for you, you sanctimonious bitch," I said, "you don't have to." I reached behind her and untied the length of rope wrapped around the tree, the leash that connected to her hands.

"Get up."

She sat in her slump. I jerked the rope, and she fell over in a heap, sniffling in the dirt. The sound of her snot woke up the voices in my head, and this time they weren't at medium volume; this time they were at full fucking throttle: *wrongwrongwrongwrong. WRONG. WRONG. WRONG. WRONG.* I wanted to scream, I wanted to throw myself in the lake right then and there, but the truth was I was too fucking scared to do it by myself. That was why she was there, why I had picked her; I was too scared to do it by myself. I jerked the rope until she cried out, and I could see her wrists were bleeding. I grabbed her by that ash blonde hair, and dear God, I was crying, I was crying, the voices were going full throttle, full decibel, and I couldn't fucking make them stop. I jerked her head back so that she could see me, my tears and her sniveling and all of it.

"You are doing this with me," I told her. "And you can thank your God for it because you are going to be a goddamn martyr, you are going to save lives by dying with me today, but you have to get this, you have to get it – I can't do this by myself. Do you get it? You have to go with me. You will go with me. I can't go by myself. And if I don't go, I will kill you and then I will kill a hundred other women because I can't fucking stop. You have to go with me."

She just stared up at me, her face and shirt covered in dirt and sweat and tears. I thought she might die right there, in my arms. She made a big heaving, sobbing noise, and bucked up, and with no thought whatsoever I smacked her in the head with my open palm. She collapsed back to the ground, sobbing.

"Oh God," she said. "Dear God."

I grabbed her by the shoulders and pulled her up to face me.

"That's right," I said, trying to push away the voices. "That's right. Think about your God. That's right."

She steadied there, watching me, and it was the longest moment of my life, one of the last; and then she nodded, crying, snot running down her face.

"Okay," she said. "Okay. What do you want me to do?"

I pulled back from her, shaking, and then reached under her armpits and pulled her to her feet. "Get in the car," I said. She looked at me again, wondering, and I shook my head. "Just get in the goddamn car."

It took the divers and the wrecker an hour to pull the Buick up. The trunk came up first, rising from the lake's surface at a crazy, canted angle. Dark water poured off the bumper. The back window had busted with the rest of them, but I couldn't see anything inside. Two round balls bobbed up beside it, and it took me a second to place them as the divers' heads. The sheriff waved them in.

"He's holding her," one of the divers said as he mounted the dock. He shrugged his tank off. "Have you ever heard of that? He's holding her like a lover."

I watched as the Buick cleared the water and the wrecker maneuvered it onto dry ground. The crime scene team swarmed around it, examining the broken windows, the busted door lock on the passenger side. They popped the trunk and dug into the wheel well, finding my stash of trinkets. From my perch in the tree I could see our bodies, black and bloated, through the back window. My head rested on the passenger seat; Lily's arm fell out the window at an unnatural angle. I waited in the silence, waited for the rustle of breeze to come carry me away, to whatever heaven or hell was waiting for me. Surely, it was time for my release. The mockingbirds and jays were silent on the branches. But – nothing. The air was still. And then, in the silence, I heard the whisper: *wrongwrongwrong.* ❦

LAST STOP ON DOWLING STREET

SCOTT WILLIAM CARTER

Frank Granger woke possessed with the feeling that someone was in his bedroom. He bolted upright in bed, his T-shirt drenched with sweat, the metallic taste of fear in his mouth, his heart pounding so hard it was a moment before he noticed it was raining outside. Not just raining but pouring, coming down like God taking a piss after a night of drinking, as his buddy Jim used to say.

His feet were tangled in a mess of sweaty sheets. Darkness suffocated his room, no moonlight, no light from the bathroom spilling in from the hall. The smell of mold was strong; his trailer always smelled like mold when it rained. A hundred miles west of Houston, surrounded by scrub grass and tumbleweed, not another neighbor within half a mile, there wasn't any light from outside without the moon. But the bathroom light being off, that bothered Frank, because he always left the light on in case he needed to take a leak in the middle of the night. Plus ever since his old buddy Jim decided to see what the mouth of a shotgun tasted like two years back, Frank liked having a light on. He couldn't say why exactly. It just seemed better that way.

Damn power must have gone out, Frank thought. Maybe it had something to do with the riots in Houston. It had been a week since that black preacher had been shot, and the damn niggers were causing trouble everywhere. His heart just would not slow down, and he peered into the darkness, trying to make out the familiar objects in his room. The darkness seemed to have shades and hues, and if he strained he thought he caught hints of his surroundings. Was that his dresser there by the closet? Was that the wicker chair in the corner? The longer he looked at where he was sure the wicker chair was, the more he was sure that there was somebody sitting in it. Frank himself never used the chair. Alice had bought it at a garage sale, saying it would be perfect for them to sit in when they put their shoes on, but she never sat in it either as far as he could remember. He had harassed her about it for years, telling her that they really should get rid of that damn chair. Then she went and died, just passing quietly in her sleep three days short of seventy, and Frank stopped caring about the chair.

But there *was* somebody sitting in the chair, something about the darkness, the complexity of it. Don't be a damn fool, he told himself. Why would somebody sneak into your house just to sit in your wicker chair? Mind playing tricks, that's all. You don't own nothing worth stealing and you keep to yourself.

Finally, as his breathing became regular, he began to ease himself down into bed. That's when he heard a sound that could only be one thing: the distinctive crackle of a body shifting in the wicker chair. He froze, his heart pounding furiously, his mouth dry and coarse like sandpaper, and stared at where he imagined the person was sitting.

"Who's there?" he said.

When there was no answer, Frank reached to turn on his bedside lamp, and it was only then that the person spoke. "Don't."

Frank jumped as if he had just been poked in the ass with a branding iron. It was a deep, hoarse voice. Christ, there was somebody in his room – *in his damn room!* He had a Colt .45 in the drawer next to his bed, and he started to move his hand toward it.

"I wouldn't do that," the man said. Then there followed the far more terrifying noise of a pistol being cocked.

The man sounded nervous. He also had a Texas accent, and there was a certain quality to it that led Frank to believe he was a nigger. Frank's mind raced as he tried to think of any niggers who would want to kill him. There had been a lot of niggers who rode his bus back in Houston, the Dowling Street route, the one that none of the other drivers wanted because it was mostly niggers. But he had never treated them badly, not really. He had to keep them in check now and then, but he had been kind to them, kinder than they deserved, really.

"I don't got no money," Frank said.

"That's not surprising."

"I don't got no gold or coins or nothing of value."

The nigger cleared his throat. "That's not why I'm here."

Frank, his fear growing, started again for the pistol at his bedside, but the nigger spoke before he had even moved his hand a few inches.

"If you persist in that idea," the nigger said, "I'll be forced to do something about it. Besides...I brought my own gun, but I thought – well, no one could trace yours back to me."

That's when Frank realized that this nigger was no petty criminal come for whatever loose change he could find; this man had an agenda. "Who are you?" he said, his constricted throat choking off the final word.

"Just somebody's husband," the nigger said.

Frank's mind, still sluggish from that late night scotch, tried to make sense of this comment. It was said with an accusatory tone. "Do I know your wife or something?" he asked.

The nigger responded with a snort. "I doubt you'd remember her, even though she rode your bus for ten years. Besides, she's dead."

"Sorry to hear that."

"Don't fucking lie to me."

It was the first time the man had raised his voice; everything else he had said had been spoken with cool detachment. The nigger sounded like one of those fancy learned types, a professor maybe. But that last bit, there was real rage in his voice, murderous rage, and Frank suddenly felt like he was falling. "Did I wrong her in some way?" he asked.

The nigger didn't answer for a long time. The rain had picked up, pinging against the metal roof. The moaning wind sounded like a woman in childbirth, full of pain and expectation.

"She's been dead for twelve years," the nigger said, his voice now a hair above a whisper. "I never thought I'd be here, you know. I'm a man of the cloth, you see. Forgive and forget, I always say. Not that I didn't have thoughts back when she died. Awful thoughts. I looked up where you lived, in that ratty apartment back in Houston. I even stood in the shadows next to the stoop and watched you come home one night. But I didn't do anything. I still had two sons. Had to think about them."

"I guess I don't – "

"Don't speak unless I tell you to speak."

The sharpness was there in the nigger's voice again. Frank couldn't believe he was being treated this way in his own home – *and by a nigger!*

He had to think of a way out of this mess. The nigger had his pistol, sure, but there was also the .22 underneath the bed. If he could find a way to roll off the bed, on the far side where he'd be out of the nigger's line of fire, maybe he could get to the shotgun in time. Then he could blow the nigger's fucking face off.

"I didn't think I was going to tell you any of this," the nigger said. "I didn't think it mattered, but now I think it does. You need to hear it. And maybe I need to say it. Then I'll do what I came to do and finally put you behind me."

Frank's eyes were beginning to adjust to the darkness. The light was still too faint to see much, but he thought he saw the peacock-like back to the wicker chair, as well as a gleam off the nigger's bald scalp.

"I'll tell you why I'm here, Frank Granger," the nigger said. "I'll tell you as plain as I can make. I'm here because you killed my wife."

"I never killed anybody," Frank said.

"Shut up. Just shut the fuck up, you hear me?" He mumbled something under his breath, then spoke more calmly. "You see what you've done to me, Granger? My whole life I served to the glory of God, and you make me nothing but a raving lunatic. I've never raised my voice in anger in my entire life, and yet you'd think it was ordinary behavior for me. But it's not. It's you. You're poison to me, Granger. That's why I've got to kill you."

Although Frank had suspected that was why the nigger was here, it was the first time the nigger had said it so bluntly. A steady pressure was building in his bladder. What he needed was a distraction – something to give him a moment to duck under the bed and fish out the shotgun. But what? *What?*

"I swear I've never hurt anyone," Frank said, trying to sound as meek as possible. He didn't mind sounding pathetic if it would get him out of this mess. There would be plenty of time for revenge later.

"Do – not – speak!" the nigger said. "I will speak my piece and you will listen, you worthless shit. You piece of crap. You... You..." He trailed off, taking a few deep breaths until he had regained his composure. "You may not know that you killed her, but you did. My wife rode your damn bus near every day for ten years, but I bet you wouldn't recognize her if I showed you a picture. I'd bet money on it. I'd bet my entire life savings."

Frank wanted to say *but a lot of people rode my bus*, but he kept silent. He didn't know how much further he could push the nigger. He sounded like he was about to snap, so he had to tread lightly. Try to think of a way to distract the nigger. He would get out of this, Frank would. He was a survivor. He wasn't going to get shot by no nigger.

The rain and the wind had slackened, allowing other sounds into the room. He heard creaking pipes, the drip from the faucet in the kitchen, the rhodie scratching against the living room window. He wished he would hear a car, but he knew that was unlikely. Right then he hated Alice for wanting to move out in the middle of godforsaken nowhere.

"I wish, just for a minute," the nigger said, "I could climb inside your mind. Then I could know if there is even one shred of decency in you. What did you do, you want to know. All right, I'll tell you. My wife, she worked as a waitress in a diner. Even though I told her not to work overtime, she thought we needed the money. We had two young sons, and I was only a lowly assistant pastor. She didn't want her sons to look like beggars, she said. She had pride that way. I used to think it was a weakness of hers, but now I don't think so."

Frank began edging himself toward the far side of the bed. The nigger seemed to be obsessed with his own story. If Frank moved ever so slowly, maybe the bastard wouldn't notice.

"She rode your bus home from work every day," the nigger continued. "Back then, my people had to pay up front, then get off and board in the back. I'm sure you remember. You were good at enforcing it. She told me how you used to throw Negroes off your bus if they got cross with you. 'It's state law,' you'd tell them. But my wife, she obeyed the rules. She was no Rosa Parks. She couldn't afford to go to jail, not with two sons and a husband who could barely put bread on the table much less pay the rent. But one day it was raining hard, and she was coming down with a cold, and maybe she wasn't thinking so clearly. Instead of getting off and reboarding, she just dropped in her coins and started for the back. You told her to get the hell off and board the way the colored are supposed to board. And she did. She did just like what you said. She was tired and sick and cold, and the rain was coming down something fierce, but she still went back outside. And that's when…"

The nigger's voice had become strained. He took a moment to gather himself, sucking in breath through his teeth. Frank had made it halfway to the other side of the bed. Just a little farther.

"That's when you pulled away from the curb and left her there," the nigger went on, his voice rising. "Yours was the last bus of the night, so she had no choice but to walk downtown where we lived. Three miles. Three miles in the pouring rain. With a fever. She told me what happened when she got home, right before she stripped off her soaked clothes and collapsed into bed. I told her I was going to track you down and give you a piece of my mind, but she said no, that you didn't matter, that you were just a little man full of hate, and that we shouldn't bother with little men. God wouldn't want it. See, I was the man of the cloth, but she was the better person. She always was."

Frank was almost there. A few more inches…

"Well, you can probably guess what happened next," the nigger said. "All that walking in the rain, she didn't have a chance. She came down with pneumonia. That night was the last time she was really coherent. Three days later, she was dead. You wouldn't believe how hard it was not to track you down and kill you right then, Granger. I wanted to do it. I was capable of doing it. But I was going to honor her last wishes. I put my faith in God. I let him guide my way. I raised my sons. I became the pastor of a church. I thought I had put you behind me."

Frank was now close enough to do the roll. Now he just needed that distraction. A pillow! He could throw a pillow at the nigger's face.

"But then one of my sons was drafted into the army," the nigger said, "and the other one joined so they could go to Vietnam together. I was against it. I told them to go to Canada instead. They didn't listen. They went off to fight together. Three months later a Colonel in uniform showed up on Sunday in my pews, his face so solemn that he didn't have to say a word. Both of them gone, just like that."

Frank slid his hands behind his head and grasped the pillow. Sweat dribbled down his forehead. His heart pounded so hard it felt as if it would burst from his chest. If this didn't work, he was finished, but it *had* to work. He was going to blow this nigger to kingdom come.

"That's about when I stopped believing in God," the nigger said. "I went on preaching for a while, pretending it wasn't so, pretending for myself just as much as for my congregation. But the belief was gone. And now I know that sometimes things happen to you, and then you just can't believe in God anymore. Some things just take away the possibility. Some people go on pretending, but they don't really believe."

The nigger shifted in his chair, and the sound made Frank freeze. When he spoke again, Frank realized that the nigger had leaned forward.

"Even then, I didn't come looking for you," the nigger said, his voice barely a whisper. "God didn't exist, but my wife did. She was out there watching me, and I had made a promise to her. I've followed you over the years, and we've got a lot in common. You've got nobody left either, just like me, and I took some satisfaction in that. I told myself at least you would die alone. And that was enough, for a while. Then you bastards killed King. You killed King, and it was like the night you left my wife in the rain was just yesterday."

Frank knew the time had come. It was now or never. He clenched the pillow with his fists and –

"What you're about to do," the nigger said, "I wouldn't do it."

Frank's body tensed. The nigger couldn't know what he was doing. Could he? "I don't know what you're talking about," he said.

"Oh, sure you do. You're thinking of throwing that pillow at my face so you can roll off the bed and get to that shotgun. It may be dark, but I can see that plain as day. Do you think I would be stupid enough to leave that shotgun for you? Do you think I'd be that dumb, when I went to all the trouble to turn off the power? Do you really think this is the first time I've been in your pitiful little shithole?"

Frank felt as if he had been shot in the heart with an arrow. All his hope was bleeding out of him. "Please don't kill me," he whined.

For a long time, the nigger didn't respond. Then Frank heard the wicker chair groan and whine, the rustle of clothing, footsteps on the floor. Panic seized him, and he scrambled for the other side of the bed. A firm hand grabbed his shoulder and spun him onto his back. He saw the nigger's dark outline, the gleam of glasses, a silvery mustache. Frank started to squirm, but then there was a gun in his mouth, shoved deep, the metal cold and pushing against the back of his mouth. He fell still, paralyzed.

"So it comes down to this," the nigger said. "You took my wife from me, and now you're gonna get what you deserve."

The barrel went deeper. He felt the man's hand pressing down on his sternum. Frank's body convulsed. His bladder let go, his crotch warm and wet, and then the tears gushed from his eyes. "Pwea..." he said, the gun making it all but impossible to talk. "Pweeeaaa...I doh waaa die..."

Frank didn't see his life pass in front of his eyes. What he did experience was an extreme heightening of the senses. The nigger was still shrouded in darkness, but he saw him better now – the protruding forehead, the depth of despair in the recessed sockets of his eyes, the leathery texture of his skin. He smelled himself, piss and alcohol, and he smelled the nigger, a musky odor mixed with the pungent vapors of drying clothing. Frank heard the creak of the loose gutter out back, the skittering of the rats under the trailer… It all came to him at once.

Then the nigger pulled the trigger.

There was a snap that Frank both heard and felt. For half a second he thought the bullet was already traveling through his mouth and out the back of his neck, but upon thinking this he realized that it couldn't be happening, because he wouldn't have been able to think at all. And then it dawned on him that although the nigger had pulled the trigger, the gun hadn't fired.

The nigger pulled the gun out of Frank's mouth. The bed squeaked and shifted as the nigger rose. Frank, unsure of what was happening, stared up at the dark blot standing over him.

"I'll have you know I was going to kill you," the nigger said. "All the way up until tonight, I was going to do it. And I'm still going to do it. You just won't know when. You see, I realized something. I realized that if I just go on and kill you, you'll never know what it's like to live the way my wife lived when she rode your bus. You may still not really know, but at least you'll get a taste of it. You'll understand what it's like to live in fear. And I swear to you, I'm coming back, and that was the only empty chamber in the gun. I may come tomorrow, or next week, or even next year, but I will come."

Frank heard the nigger's footsteps. They were loud at first, and then they were muffled by the wall between the bedroom and the hall. The front door slammed. Footsteps on the gravel. And then nothing.

He lay completely immobile in bed, the piss drying on his body, the taste of metal still lingering in his mouth. The rain had picked up again, the wind, too. He knew he had to get up and do something about the power. Go find the circuit box and see if he could get the lights back on. He couldn't just lay there in the dark. It was making him crazy.

But Frank couldn't get himself to move. The nigger might be out there. He might be waiting for him, just giving him a bit of false hope before he took that hope away. His fear was paralyzing him. No, Frank thought. The nigger wouldn't kill him tonight. Maybe tomorrow, but not tonight. It wouldn't make sense for the nigger to let him live, only to shoot him a few minutes later.

And then an even more troubling thought occurred to Frank.

He realized there was a good chance this nigger was not the only one who wanted to kill him.

YOU WILL BE WEARING GREEN

DANIEL BENNETT

A gang of teenagers sat laughing around a mobile phone on the 18:17 out of Victoria, but Derek tried to ignore them. He concentrated on his paper, reading the front page story about a body found in woodland on the outskirts of the city, a young female student who had been missing for over a week. Beyond the train window, the interior of the station drained away, soon replaced by the steel-crossed view over the Thames.

At Balham, the seat beside him was vacated, and a young woman sat down, brushing against Derek's leg as she moved past him. She was in her late twenties, a plain, ordinary looking woman with a narrow face, and a thin pointed nose turned up at the end. She sniffed constantly, and the nostril nearest to Derek was pink; she had a light cold. As she looked hopelessly through the contents of her bag for something to wipe her nose, Derek retrieved the pack of tissues he kept in his suit jacket pocket. He acted quickly, to ignore the growing feeling of doubt.

"Excuse me..."

The woman lifted her eyes. As Derek was about to continue, a man's sex cries cut into the quiet of the carriage. The teenagers cackled, turning up the volume on the mobile phone. For a second Derek and the woman stared at one another as the noise intensified, mixing commands and profanities. The woman looked away, and shifted slightly in her seat. Derek stared back down at the newspaper. The woman left at Streatham Hill. Derek carried on to West Norwood. The teenagers were still laughing when he left the train.

Recently, Derek's life had reached a state of crisis. A quiet, stolid man, he tended to occupy himself with whatever was placed in front of him, as long as what was placed in front of him was not human. Most of his relationships had been started by desperation or drunkenness; usually it was both. "We're moving in different directions," his last girlfriend, Carol, had explained to him, a year before. "You want things…I want things. They aren't the same things. I'll always think of you fondly." It was clear that she had found someone else. Although the relationship had never been happy, the regular sex had been a welcome distraction. Now that it had gone…it was a very frustrating time. There were ways of dealing with his situation – he had the internet, and full cable access – but these outlets seemed to make things worse. Eventually, he mentioned it to Sneddon.

They worked together in the complaints centre of a travel agents. It was a Friday afternoon. The phones were dead, the post brought nothing but circulars, the only email was spam from Nigeria. Across from the partitioned desks which Derek and Sneddon shared, a cardboard backdrop showed a blonde woman in a white bikini, reclining on a sun-lounger. Not a day would go past without Sneddon making a comment about this picture.

"They expect us to be bloody monks," he said, staring up at the woman's tinted smile. "It's just such a bloody distraction." Fake tanned, the tips of his brown hair highlighted blond, Sneddon sat back heavily in his chair, sucking on a lollipop. Ever since quitting smoking the month before, he ate as many as ten lollipops a day.

"I know what you mean," Derek agreed.

"I'll tell you what, when I go out tonight, some little tart is going to pay for this." Sneddon's voice rasped around the bowl of the lollipop, spittle gathering in the corners of his mouth. "It's been two weeks since that night in Stepney, and that's two weeks too long."

Derek laughed. "God, it's been longer than that for me…"

"Since Carol? Christ, that was *a year* ago." He stared over pityingly. "You should have come to me sooner."

It was true. Sneddon was a man to be admired. On the desktop of his computer, he had saved a picture: a bridge crossing a ravine of savage, orange rock. A line hung down into the maw of the ravine. From the line hung a man, dressed in white helmet, a red T-shirt, blue shorts. Sneddon was that man. He moved across and perched upon Derek's desk; he seemed genuinely pleased to be able to help.

"I can see that I'm going to have to explain a few things to you." Sneddon paused and sucked on his lollipop, composing himself for what was obviously going to be an important lecture. "The world is made up of many layers," he began. "Underworlds, subcultures, you can call them what you like. You and I, Derek, you and I live near the surface. We are honest citizens, taxpayers, homeowners, we drive our cars, we watch our TVs. We are the wheels of society.

"But often we have to move from our level to the one below. This can happen for a number of reasons. In years before this could be fraught with danger. Sometimes risks were punished. Do you know why?" Derek shook his head. "I'll tell you: it was because the space between the layers was too great." He illustrated the gap holding his palms parallel to one another. "People, unwitting people who wanted to cross between the worlds, they fell through the gap."

"What happened to them?"

Sneddon scowled at the question. "The point is that now, these layers are closer to the surface." He gestured to the computer behind him. "And all you need is this."

"I won't pay for it," Derek whispered.

"Who said anything about paying? You're stuck in the old way of thinking." Sneddon regarded Derek with pity. "Your problem is a lack of confidence. I've seen it so many times before." He gestured at the poster. "You see a girl like that, you want her, but you imagine she will never want you." He shook his head, took the lollipop from his mouth, and let it bounce in front of Derek's face, like a majorette's baton. "You need to realise: women have the same needs as men."

Sneddon sent him away with a couple of internet sites, and Derek began his search that evening, sitting at the computer in his front room. Eventually, he found a site advertising services for people around South London. It described itself as a singles agency, but the explicit images and text made it clear that no one was looking for a life partner. After paying a month's subscription, he registered as Robert Bower, deciding that it was only sensible to use a pseudonym. The name belonged to a man who had taken his family on holiday to a resort in Durban. A sewage pipe had cracked underneath the Olympic sized pool, sending raw human shit gushing into the pool while Robert Bower and his family had been swimming. Robert Bower had been understandably unimpressed, and had expressed himself to Derek very forcibly by letter and by phone. When Derek thought of the acts Robert Bower would soon perform with untold numbers of strange women, it seemed like better compensation than the refund and travel vouchers which he had actually demanded.

Unfortunately, those early experiences were disappointing. Every night, Derek would receive emails from a number of women in his area. After a few introductions, things became more heated. These exchanges could be stimulating, but it was hard to escape the sense of desperation. He had expected the website to provide him with something from his fantasies, but when it came time for swapping photographs, his interest faded. These were lonely, desperate women, as lonely and desperate, Derek realised, as himself. When Sneddon began to question him at work, Derek told him that yes, everything was fine, more than fine, that he was involved in the most exciting period of his life. The truth was that he found himself disillusioned, almost humiliated.

It was then that he heard from Janice. From the moment he received her first email, he was captivated; her photos were overwhelming. In her mid-twenties, she was attractive, with a narrow face framed by straight glossy black hair, a lithe muscular body. In one picture, she lay back on a bright red bedspread wearing a black silk nightdress. In another, she posed by an indoor swimming pool in a bikini of electric blue. The photographs looked professional, artistic. She was exactly the kind of woman who Derek had imagined for himself. The tone of her messages was confident and sensual, but there was also a hint of danger. "Hi Robert," one read. "I see you want to play. Tell me what you want me to do." Derek sent back an email, similar in tone to those he had shared with some of the other women on the site, but Janice was unimpressed. "Not good enough at all," she wrote back. "I want something *harder*."

It took Derek a while to reply. He stayed up until two in the morning, writing and deleting, drinking a few cans of beer. He clicked through a few websites. He walked to his bedroom and retrieved a photograph of Carol. He put everything into the message, his hurt and frustration, his need. It was the angriest, most honest thing he had written in his entire life, and the next morning, he hardly dared turn on the computer. When he did, he found a message waiting for him. "Foreplay is over," the subject field read. The text of the body gave instructions for where they would meet: next Saturday, on the high street in Bromley. Derek would collect Janice from the high street, outside a large chemists. "I can promise you the time of your life."

That morning, he showered, soaping himself with a gel fragranced with menthol and vanilla. He shaved with care and precision, clipping excess hairs from his nostrils with a small pair of silver scissors, filing his fingernails. He dressed and ate breakfast; it was still two hours until he had to meet Janice. The life that had been opened up to him – this subculture, as Sneddon had called it – felt more comforting than he could have imagined. If this works out, he told himself, it is quite possible that I will have achieved happiness. I have a decent home. My job is an irritation at times, but the money is acceptable. If this part of my life is made complete, it is quite possible that I will never want for anything again.

For a while, he watched the television news. The presenter talked about the war, about a disaster in Africa, a fire in a monastery outside Barcelona, the continuing investigation into the death of the young woman outside the city. Her picture appeared on the screen, her delicate face and bobbed black hair. She was smiling, leaning back on a rusted iron gate over which the head of a Friesian cow appeared. The newsreader gave a short account of the woman's actions on the day she had disappeared, describing her clothing, her movements. Derek hardly paid attention, flicking through the Sunday supplement for the TV listings.

When the time came, he headed out to Bromley, listening to his favourite radio station, watching women as they walked along the pavements. Some of them, he thought, might one day be available to Robert Bower. The idea gave him a sense of purpose, of power. Soon he reached the outskirts of Bromley; the traffic moved slowly along the high street. When Derek saw the sign for the chemists, he slowed down the car, looking for a place where he could pull up to the kerb. He recognised Janice immediately. She was standing a few metres away from the entrance to the shop, a lithe woman, much taller than he had imagined. She wore her tar black hair in a sharp bob, blue jeans and trainers, a black shirt and a brown corduroy jacket over the top. Derek was a little disappointed with her clothes: he had expected something more alluring, dangerous, erotic. As she approached the car, he leaned over to open the passenger door.

"Hello, is that Robert?" Her voice was high pitched with a Northern accent.

"That's right. Janice?"

Janice climbed into the front seat. "Can't be too careful, these days." She closed the door behind her and they sat facing each other. "Well." She laughed nervously, and leant over to kiss Derek on the mouth. "Nice to finally meet you." Her skin smelled of a subtle, musky deodorant, her breath of mint and cigarette smoke. "Well, come on then. Let's go."

Derek eased the car into the flow of traffic. He could hardly keep his eyes on the road. "So where do you come from? Your accent..."

Janice nodded. "Huddersfield. I've been down here for a while now." She glanced at the passenger window, which was open halfway down. "Do you mind if I close this? I don't want to mess up my hair."

"Of course."

As the window closed, the sound of the high street cut out, and they were sealed in together. Janice looked back over at Derek, biting her lip as she smiled. "God though, I'm looking forward to this."

"Me too."

"I swear I haven't been able to keep my mind on anything else."

"Me neither."

"I thought we'd drive to a place I know. Outdoors."

"Whereabouts?"

"It's a bit of woodland I know. Very private. Would you like that?"

"Yes, of course." Derek frowned up at the sky through the windscreen. "Looks a bit cloudy though."

"The country air," Janice said. "It keeps you healthy."

"Might rain."

She laughed. "Nothing like the feel of rain on your skin."

They trailed through satellite towns and their outskirts, finally breaking free into the countryside, the bland scrub fields, a huge power station dominating the horizon. Derek flicked on the radio, and they chatted about their lives. Janice had moved down to London after splitting from her husband. She worked in the offices of a bank in the City, a job which she hated, but which had a lot of benefits. At first Derek had been worried that she would be disappointed with him, and that she would find some excuse not to go through with things. She seemed totally relaxed in his company, however, and sat back in her seat, her eyes rarely leaving his face, laughing warmly at his jokes.

They had been driving for half an hour when they passed through a large village. It was nothing remarkable: a green, a stream, a pub, a bank of shops, a decaying church sliding slowly into moss. The name zipped past them on a white sign. "I know that place," he said, more to himself than to Janice. She nodded absently, without looking over at him.

"Been here before?"

"No. Not at all."

"It's not far now," Janice said. "Take the next right."

She directed Derek down a narrow road amongst a small patch of pine woodland. The trees arched over the road, obscuring the sky. He pulled the car off the road onto a pitted dirt track, parking it away from the road. "After all," Janice explained. "We don't want to attract attention." Outside, she took Derek's hand, and they walked into the woods. The smell of pine needles was strong in the air. The ground was littered with old crisp packets and beer cans; not far from where he had parked the car, Derek noticed a small length of torn police tape wound tightly to the trunk of a tree. The sunlight shattered on the ground beneath the leaves, the shadows oozing in freckled patterns to the soft beat of the trees. It was a peaceful scene, but Derek could hardly have been more agitated: his pulse throbbed thickly in his neck, his breathing was shallow and expectant. A bird clattered through the branches. As they reached the centre of a small clearing, Janice pulled at Derek's hand.

"I think this is far enough."

She moved close to him, and they began to kiss, her small teeth nibbling at his lips. She unbuttoned the top three buttons of her blouse, and pulled down her jeans. "I want you to keep your clothes on," she said. "For now, at least." The blouse hung down to her thighs like a short dress. Derek watched openly as Janice reached underneath and removed her underwear, scrunching them into a ball, and letting them drop onto the forest floor. Derek's hands were shaking slightly. His fingers struggled on his belt.

"I'd better help you with that." Janice bent down and pulled at the tongue of his leather belt, at the zip of his fly. A cool subtle breeze blew through the woods, catching the skin on the back of Derek's neck. The warmth of Janice's mouth enclosed him, and he experienced a sense of vertiginous elation. It was the most intense, the most perfect moment of his life.

They fell down to the ground. Twigs cracked under the pressure of their bodies, dried leaves rasped. At one stage, Janice rolled away and scrambled inside her handbag, removing a wall plug attached to a long length of flex. She rolled back towards him and pushed the flex into his hands.

"Tie me up." Obediently, Derek bent down and wrapped the plug around her wrists. "Not like that," Janice insisted. "It needs to be tighter."

"I'm sorry." He pulled as hard as he could.

"That's good," she gasped. "That's perfect. Now roll me onto my front."

As they continued, Derek reached out for Janice's hair, but she pushed his hand away. It was only then that he noticed she wore a wig: that under the line of black her blonde hair was crushed beneath a finely meshed net. He lost his rhythm for a second.

"You're not done are you?" Janice called out.

"No."

"Good. Now put your hands around my neck." Janice spoke to him patiently but firmly. "Do it now."

"Like this?"

"That's good. Now tighter. Do it tighter. Don't finish but... Steady. Yes. That's right."

A bird was singing somewhere in the trees. As he lay upon his back, Derek concentrated on the mellifluence of the song. He would have liked to see the bird, or even better to be able to name it from the call; he felt very content. Eventually, the song subsided. Janice stood up and began to dress, brushing twigs and shreds of leaf from her clothes. Derek watched her from the ground, feeling a sense of heightened contentment, where sensations of the cool breeze on his skin, the dampness in the air, the slight pain of the twigs and stones on the forest floor pushing into his back, made up the quiet ecstasy of life. As she did up the belt on her jeans, Janice stared away from him, towards a cluster of bushes on the edge of the clearing. She was beautiful, utterly beautiful. There were many things that he would like to have said.

Just as he was about to speak, the bushes parted, and a figure appeared from amongst them. He was a dark, rangy man dressed in blue denim and leather. He wore a pair of circular spectacles and carried a camcorder. Janice walked over to meet him, and, without a word, took the camcorder from his hands. "Be seated," the man said as Derek moved to stand. "My name is Star. What's your name, friend?"

"Derek." It would take him minutes to realise that he had used his real name.

"Derek," Star said. "It is good to meet you."

Even though Janice had started filming their conversation, the first thing that occurred to Derek was that this was a robbery. "I haven't got any money," he stammered. "I haven't got *anything*."

Star nodded, as though this had been expected. "Then you are a man like myself."

The name of the village returned to him. Details from the newspaper article about the murder in the woodlands returned to him. He thought of the police tape wound around the tree, a few metres away from where they were now standing.

"The woman," he said. "The dead woman..."

Star shook his head. "I mourn for the unfortunates. She was taken young. The monster that could commit such a crime... There are no words to express my hatred." Star paused. He touched his lips with the fingers of his right hand and glanced above him, where the thin network of the bare trees ran against the sky. "I want you to understand, Derek," he said eventually, "I am only a service."

"A service?"

"The world is unhappy, and hungry," Star continued, pacing around the clearing. "And its needs are manifold. People see what happens to such unfortunates and they grieve for their passing. They demand justice, the only justice they understand. I can't begin to debate the right or wrong of their needs. Raise arguments about the illusion of justice, and I'd probably agree with you. Nature has no concept of such a thing. It's only a dream, which remains constant as people's values change. When people were religious, justice was God. When people embraced money, justice became compensation." He shook his head. "These things we think we can buy..."

Janice continued to film Derek, occasionally moving the camera over to Star. She had removed the wig and hairnet, and her dull blonde hair hung down to her shoulders. At first, Derek had been scared, but the presence of the camera put him at ease. I've been set up, he thought, an extreme practical joke for a reality TV show. It was the only explanation. He glanced at the camera, and forced a nervous smile.

"Do you ever stop to consider," Star went on, "that once money became divorced from man's ability to pull a precious metal from the ground, then the last trace of its true value disappeared. Did you ever think of money as only paper and numbers? Have you ever looked at the stock market and seen only code? We trade with an illusion, but we expect value. Did you ever consider that once you pay for something, you reduce its value, that in fact, you destroy it. All we are doing with the current system of economics is to take things – real things of substance, that you can touch and hold and feel, and disintegrate them into an idea. That is all money is: an idea. Information transmitted between corporations who view us only as a means to keep the information flowing. Notional, even more notional than the relationship between a word and a thing.

"What disturbs me," Star went on, "is that I can see all of this, that I know it to be true, but I know that I am powerless. I am only weak." He leaned back and stared at the sky beyond the trees. "People demand justice. Even if that justice is a show, a sham, a performance, just another example of the way people confuse media with life. People want justice. So I provide justice."

And saying that, he produced a small, silver automatic from the pocket of his jacket, took careful aim, and shot Derek twice through the head. Derek collapsed to the floor, shuddering once, with his arm bent underneath his body. The bullet wounds stood out bright and rude on his forehead. Janice let the camera linger on them for a few seconds before turning off the camera and replacing the lens cap. She walked over to Star's side, as he replaced the pistol in the pocket of his jacket.

"How was it?" she asked. "The early part." All trace of her Northern accent had disappeared.

"It was good," Star said. "You were perfect."

"I thought he would never get it right. He was so slow."

"He *was* slow," Star said, "but you guided him well. You took the lead, honey."

Her face soured. "Please, don't call me that."

Star grinned. "I only do it because it upsets you."

"Why do you like to upset me?"

"I like to watch your eyebrows when they rise."

"You like to watch me, period."

"Lisa," Star said, with his hand upon his heart, "I think the world is only a theatre for you."

After Star directed Lisa in a few more shots – a close up of the corpse's face, during which a fly landed upon the right eyeball, capturing the light on the halo of congealing blood which had formed beneath the head – they walked back to the bushes, retrieved two spades, and set about digging a grave. They took turns in filming the process, letting the camera linger on the pale, stricken face as it was dusted and eventually covered with the grey forest soil, to be further covered with grass and moss. Lisa shot a tight close up of Star's boot pressing the earth upon the body.

He had parked his car on a dirt track leading up from the road. They walked in silence; he had hardly even acknowledged her since they buried the body, preoccupied, she guessed, with the work still to be done on the film. When they reached the car, he removed the DAT player and microphone from his jacket which he had used to record his monologues, which he regarded as integral to the films. Since they had first started working together she had listened to many similar diatribes, but she couldn't help but feel that Star was deluding himself. A few artistic close ups were one thing – Lisa, after all, was fond of this aspect of the films – but when it came to lengthy philosophising, the genre didn't need that kind of decoration. She kept her thoughts to herself, however. It was best not to argue with Star.

As he unlocked the driver's door, and tossed the player onto the passenger seat, Lisa looked out over the field beyond. A dead crow had been trussed up on wire, presumably by the farmer, to scare off birds from a row of new seeds. Removing the lens cap from the camera, she shot ten, fifteen seconds of the bird, as it rocked on its wires in the breeze, the wings spread out in a gruesome mockery of flight.

"What are you doing?" By the tone of his voice, she knew that he was unhappy.

"I thought it would look good," she replied. "We could use it at the very end, after we've buried him."

As she turned to face him, her reflection warped to the surface of his glasses. Star held out his hand, only breaking a smile once Lisa had passed him the camera. As he turned back towards the car, he tapped his free palm idly against her cheek. "It's my vision, honey," he murmured, softly. "Remember that. It's what *I* want to see."

He left Lisa to collect the victim's car, driving on ahead because he was anxious to get back to the Essex farmhouse where he had set up his editing suite. As always, trust was the long leash on which he allowed her to run. Lisa took her time as she walked back to the car. Under the cover of the trees, the air was chilly. The costume of the murdered girl felt uncomfortable, and her head itched from being under the wig. While she felt slightly used, she knew that the only remaining traces of the latest victim would vanish after a hot bath and brandy. She lit a cigarette, the way she always did, after sex, after a death. Star didn't like her to smoke in his company.

Inside the car, she sat for a moment in the driver's seat, Star's presence so dominant that he might have been sitting right beside her. He was the most depraved, intimidating, intelligent man she had ever known. What experiences had resulted in the idea for these films, what agenda he worked through, the names which constituted the great grave secret of his client base, she had only a vague idea. It didn't really concern her. When Star had offered the opportunity to avenge a life which sometimes seemed like only a succession of abuses, she had followed him. If he had snared her, she had been snared for a long time before she had met him, and her life with him felt like an escape. Through the betrayal and theatre of their enterprise, she had discovered part of herself that she had never known, and it was all the more intriguing and affirming because it was an absence, a vacancy.

Always, always Star. As she fired the ignition, and set the car rolling through the woods – the day growing dark under the cloudy sky, growing cold – back to the road on which she would trace Star's trail, she allowed herself her usual rebellion. Thinking maybe it was time she set out by herself. Thinking that life is too short to agree to the roles people make you play. Thinking, dreaming that, maybe, the next film that Star would feature in would be his own. Thinking that, anyway, she would have to run from him: because one day, she was sure, Star would want someone younger to help occupy his time. Someone who through innocence, willingness or vitality, could help him postpone the moment when death would come for him, hungry and inexorable, without justice or sympathy, but still with its own uncomprehending innocence – the way, she decided, it came for everyone.

Lisa shook her head, and screwed out her cigarette in the ashtray. The road stood waiting for her at the end of the pitted forest track. She ought to keep her mind on driving. It must have been at least fifty miles back to the cottage; she had no idea which way to go.　　　　　॥

A HANDFUL OF DUST

IAN R. FAULKNER

"I have to show you this," Steven Williams said.

"What is it?"

"It's my wife."

"Sorry?" Matthew Hadley frowned, confused, and looked up from the photograph Williams had just handed him.

"It's my wife," the man repeated, nodding to indicate the grainy, slightly out of focus image. "I took it on her last day here."

"I..." Matthew began; then, inanely repeating the phrase for the third time, said, "Your wife?"

"It's amazing isn't it? I just had to show you. You've been so kind and understanding, I just knew you would appreciate seeing Emma."

The five by seven print Matthew held appeared almost abstract at first glance. It had been shot at an oblique angle and, given the white glare of reflected flash that washed out the upper right hand corner, probably through glass. It showed a dark, cramped space, filled to capacity by an oblong polished surface, and rising from deeper, blue-black shadows in the foreground, a burst of overexposed yellow that faded to become a red mist at the top left.

"I had to obtain special permission from the crematorium to be able to view Emma's departure. They have a little hatch in the door of the crematory they use for inspection and I was able to look through it and watch as Emma left. When the flames took hold and I saw her, I had to take a picture."

Wide-eyed and suddenly icy cold, Matthew looked up at Williams. "This is your..." His throat felt clogged with ash and he had to swallow repeatedly before he could finish. "This is your wife." It seemed to be all he could say.

He looked back down at the picture.

"Yes. It's her soul," Williams said, oblivious to Matthew's distaste and distress. "If you look closely you can see Emma's face in the smoke."

Williams leaned across the coffee table between them and tapped the red mist in the photograph: focusing Matthew's attention.

"Do you see?" he asked.

Matthew stared, unable to look away. His chest hurt. He couldn't seem to draw in enough air. The ice of moments ago had melted and he now felt uncomfortably warm. Sweat beaded on his brow and ran down his sides under his shirt.

"Can you see her smiling?" Williams asked. "Can you see?"

He could. Oh God. He could. There was a face in the smoke, but... but...

His fingers opened and the photograph dropped to the table. It landed face up next to Matthew's almost empty teacup: the dregs at the bottom undrinkable with tea leaves. His mouth felt lined with them, thick with their taste. The awful photo refused to release him. Even now he couldn't look away.

"I feel so much better knowing Emma's gone on to a better place."

If he hadn't been seated in the recliner opposite Williams, if he'd been standing, Matthew knew he would have fallen. He didn't believe his legs would support him right now. He reached out and gingerly slid the photograph across the table's surface to Williams.

"You *do* think she's gone to a better place, don't you?" Williams asked, picking up the print and looking longingly, lovingly, at the morbid image. "You do, don't you, Matthew?"

"I'm..." Matthew didn't know what to say. "I'm sure she has."

Williams smiled a melancholic smile. "I still talk to Emma, you know?"

Matthew nodded.

"Even knowing she has moved on, I still miss her. I try not to be sad, because I know she wouldn't want me to be unhappy, but it's hard sometimes. That's why I used the insurance money to buy the Jeep. It's something we'd always wanted and... Well, I just knew I was doing the right thing when I met you, Matthew."

The brand new, top of the range Jeep Cherokee was the reason for Matthew being at Williams's house. He had agreed to deliver the vehicle personally. He had felt sorry for the man and thought it the least he could do. After all, Williams had enough on his plate: the man had lost his new wife from cancer at age thirty-two and been left with two young boys to bring up.

When Matthew had first approached Williams to ask if he could help him, the man had already shuffled around the showroom a good half dozen times, his two young boys in tow, and, at Matthew's words, he had burst into tears. Over coffee he had told Matthew the tale of his wife's dying wish: to own a four-by-four Jeep Cherokee, and Matthew's heart had gone out to the man and his family.

"I..." Matthew licked his lips. "I have to go, Mr Williams."

"Steven, please."

"Steven. I have to go." Matthew stood up. He wanted out of the man's house. It didn't matter if Bruce Jones wasn't due to pick him up for another twenty minutes, there was no way he was going to wait around making small talk with Williams. The man needed help. "I have to get back to the garage," he said. "I hope everything works out for you."

"I'm sure it will, but thank you Matthew."

At the front door, Matthew turned and conditioning made him reach out and take Williams's proffered hand. "Take care of yourself Matthew," Williams said, holding on to Matthew's hand. "I hope you never lose anyone you love. It's an awful thing and so terribly lonely."

Now Matthew felt a complete heel for being so insensitive and judgemental. Okay, the photograph wasn't right, but it had only been a matter of weeks since the man had lost his wife.

"At least you have the kids," Matthew said.

"Yes. David and Jonathan are Godsends, although I think they'll be living with their father now Emma's gone."

"I'm sorry. I didn't realise..."

"Yes, they're from Emma's first marriage. I wish they *could* stay with me, as they remind me so much of Emma they keep her alive in my mind, but I don't think their father will allow it. Still, even without the boys, I'll never forget her."

"God no, of course you won't. She'll always be with you."

"I know she will," Williams said. "I've made sure of that. I eat a teaspoonful of her everyday. We'll never be separated again. She'll always be a part of me."

The shock of what Williams said made Matthew's jaw drop open in a perfect O.

"The ashes don't taste too bad," the man continued, gaze locked on the ground and oblivious to Matthew's reaction. "I just think of them dissolving inside me; joining my bloodstream, you know? It *is* Emma's essence, after all: her earthly remains." Williams looked up as Matthew pulled his hand out of Williams's grip.

"You don't think it's too strange do you?" the man asked.

"Oh no," Matthew said, backing away. "Not at all. I think it's a…a…a romantic thing to do."

"I knew you'd understand." Williams beamed. "I just knew you would understand."

"I don't believe it!" Matthew exclaimed.

"You say something, love?" Katherine Ellis called from the hallway of their home.

"It's him. It's Doctor Death."

"What? Who's Doctor Death?" Katherine asked, walking into the kitchen.

"It's him," Matthew said. "In the paper. God, I don't believe it. I said he was mad as a hatter."

"Who's mad as a hatter?" Katherine frowned, concerned by Matthew's agitation, and crossed to stand beside him.

He slapped the open newspaper down on the kitchen table next to his breakfast plate and mug of tea, and tapped his finger on the photograph under the headline. "Him. Him."

"But who is he?" Katherine asked, confused and worried.

"You remember me telling you about that guy I sold a Jeep to, who had photographed his wife being cremated, and who was eating a spoonful of her ashes each day? It would have been about eighteen months ago."

"That's him?"

"That's him! Steven Williams. Doctor Death!"

"You're sure?" Katherine asked, angling the paper towards her so she could read the article.

"Oh yeah. It's definitely him."

"Oh my God. It says here he – "

"Killed his two kids," Matthew finished. "I know." He twisted the paper back around away from Katherine. "He beat them both to death in the back of his parked car with a claw hammer. They were on their way to school and he just pulled over and started hitting them."

"Didn't you meet his kids?" Katherine asked.

"I did, but I don't think it's the same ones." Matthew scanned the print. "Yeah, here it is," he said, "it says 'Steven Williams, a 39-year-old unemployed IT professional, was found guilty by a jury at Birmingham Crown Court of murdering his stepson Gary, ten, and his stepdaughter Chelsea, eight, with a claw hammer.'"

"And?"

"The kids I met were both boys. I seem to remember him saying they were going to live with their father, or something like that."

"Jesus."

"I know. I mean..." Matthew shook his head, lost for words.

Again Katherine pulled the paper away from Matthew. "You're right. Listen to this: 'Williams was also found guilty of causing actual bodily harm to his common-law wife and mother to the two children, Galina Vasilieva.'" She read some more, then said, "Here you go: 'Twenty minutes after he had left Galina he telephoned her to tell her that he had killed the children. He then telephoned his eldest son from his previous marriage before phoning the emergency services.'"

"What should I do?" Matthew asked.

"Nothing," Katherine said. "It's got nothing to do with you."

On his way to work Matthew stopped off and picked up all the morning editions. Each paper contained a slight variation on the story and, seated at his desk, Matthew read and reread each of the articles until he began to piece together what had happened. He was amazed he had not picked up on the story before now. It must have been in the papers for weeks.

Matthew picked up another newspaper.

It seemed Williams had telephoned the emergency services three times before the police found the battered bodies of Gary and Chelsea and arrested him. On each occasion he had given a different story and the jury had heard all three tapes. During the first call to the operator, Williams admitted that he had just killed his kids and said that he was going to kill himself. He confided that his wife Galina had left him and said: "I've killed the kids. They're at the side of me." He then claimed his pulse was getting weak, adding: "I have stabbed myself...in my throat."

The second call had Williams claiming that Albanian gunmen had killed his stepchildren, because Galina had stolen money from the brothel where she worked as a prostitute.

Throughout his final call Williams had sobbed continuously, which had made it difficult for the operator to follow, but the gist of the call was that, apparently, his ex-wife, Emma, had made him do it because she was jealous; because he didn't love her any more; because he had given away her sons.

This final call was the most disturbing in many ways for Matthew. It brought back his memory of the photograph Williams had shown him, made him remember his first impression of the image captured by the chemicals in the film.

Matthew didn't sleep well that night. He was plagued by nightmares that left him exhausted and ill at ease. Each horror was worse than the last, filled with brutality and death, and in all of them Katherine died, viciously, by his hands.

"You need to see a doctor, Matthew," Katherine said as she breezed into the kitchen. "You look awful, love."

"I'm just tired. That's all. I'm still not sleeping too well." Matthew looked away from Katherine and focused on eating his toast. He didn't want her to see the lie in his eyes.

In truth, Matthew hadn't had an undisturbed night for over a month, ever since he had read the newspaper reports of Steven Williams's trial and he remembered the day he had delivered the man his new Jeep Cherokee.

"You don't have to tell me," she said with a smile to take the sting from her words. "I'm in the same bed, remember?"

"I'm sorry. It's just..." he started, but couldn't finish. He didn't want to tell her any more untruths.

"Just what, love? What is it? You know you can tell me."

He shook his head, weary beyond belief and words. That was the problem: he could not tell Katherine what was wrong. She deserved more. Better. Matthew felt disgusted by the things he dreamed of lately and he was sure Katherine would hate him if she ever knew of the things he saw himself doing to her in his nightmares.

"It's nothing," he said, breaking his promise. "I'll ring and make an appointment to see Dr Hartford today. If nothing else, at least she can give me something to help me sleep."

"Make sure you do, love. I worry about you, you know?"

She kissed him on the top of his head. "I'll see you later. Have a good day."

"You too," he said, standing up from the table and following Katherine to the front door. "Don't work too hard."

"I won't," she said with a wave.

He picked up the morning paper from the mat, shut the door, and walked back to the table to finish his breakfast. Maybe having a day off would help? Couldn't hurt anyway.

Matthew sat down and unfolded the paper.

The headline stopped his breath.

Steven Williams was dead.

A fellow inmate had found Williams in his cell at Blakenhurst Prison. He had hung himself with his shoelaces from the upturned end of his bed. A suicide note had been pinned to his shirt protesting his innocence and stating he was going to join his dead children in heaven.

"Jesus!" Matthew yelped, as the thump of the letterbox made him jump. He put the paper down, his heart beating wildly, and went to collect the post.

Back at the table his mind replayed the news story, as he flipped through the morning mail, tossing aside the junk and opening bills. For some reason the journalist had reiterated something the judge had said at the end of Williams's trial. The reporter had written that Mr Justice King had told Williams it was a 'wicked' thing he had done in order to 'spite his wife' and for an inexplicable reason these words troubled Matthew.

The last piece of post was a letter addressed to him. It was in a pale blue envelope and appeared to have been posted the day before. The address label was printed by hand in blue biro; the postmark identified it as having come from Redditch.

Matthew slit the top open with his finger and removed the single sheet of lined notepaper. It looked like it had been ripped from a spiral notebook and was written in the same blue printed handwriting as the envelope.

Dear Matthew, it began.

I am so sorry for what I have done. I only hope my death makes amends for everything. You were so kind to me, so understanding, I only wanted you to know what Emma was like. To feel the love we shared. I only wanted you to experience what a wonderful person I thought she was, but I know now what I did was wrong. I was wrong. I am so sorry. I am so very sorry.

Yours truly,

Steven Williams

Matthew felt like he had been punched.

The note dropped to the table. He picked up his mug and drained the last of his lukewarm tea, and, as his mouth filled with tea leaves, Matthew realised with horror why the sensation terrified him so much.

His throat clogged with ashes.

THINKING OF ALICE

ROBERT WESTON

◦⟨ **G** ⟩◦

Daniel Holloway wore his lesions like mink. From what I could see – not much more than his face and hands – it was safe to say his whole body was covered. An attendant, dressed more like a barrister than a wet nurse, stood at Holloway's bedside in a suffocating tweed suit, leather portfolio tucked under his arm like a medical chart. This therapeutic banker, I knew, was Yates. When Holloway spoke, I saw even his tongue was afflicted. "Slthee-akeh?" he said. I looked to Steve. He was as perplexed as I was. Yates leaned into his master's face – not too close, mind you – and in a moist whisper, Holloway repeated himself. Yates appeared to get it. "Mr Holloway would like to know if you are *okay*?"

Suddenly, understandably, I was concerned for my health. "Me? I'm fine. What do you mean, 'am I okay'?"

Yates ignored me; he was tremendously adept at making people feel transparent. Steve, however, was simply too big to miss. Besides, he and Yates had met before (Steve had only ever referred to him as "that skinny bastard").

"So," Yates said, "is he okay?"

Steve shrugged his bull shoulders, limp and careless. "He's okay, sure. He's with me. He's fine."

Yates blinked. "Good. Please, come in." And so we were invited into the seventh and the largest room in the Hard Rock Hotel's Elvis Suite, the priciest in the building. "As is evident," said Yates, "my employer – soon to be your employer – isn't entirely well. Both strains of cellulitis and staphylococcus are fully antibiotic-resistant. Daniel Holloway, I regret to admit, and much to our organization's chagrin, will be gone in a matter of days." Yates spoke as if Holloway wasn't in the room. In a fairly upsetting way, he barely was. Even still, his eyes were alert. They darted between Steve, Yates and me, but that looked to be as much communication as he could muster; the most expressive noises came from his chest – pops and gurgles of phlegm and whatever else was down there. So maybe Yates was right, maybe the third-person treatment was called for. "Our organization has always been known for its resourcefulness, and although traditional methods may have failed, we believe a more radical treatment may be open to us."

Steve shifted his weight. "The Black Box," he said. I could hear the grin on his face.

Yates gave Steve a long look. "We'd very much prefer if you could refrain from making direct reference to the object."

I nodded. "Sure, sure." There was no disguising the obsequiousness in my voice. I felt pitiful hearing it.

And once again, Yates ignored me. "Research indicates that in its present housing the device is too small to be of use to Mr Holloway personally, but we believe the basic technology is transferable, provided you can provide us with a prototype."

Steve looked out the window. "The guy's a stage magician, right? So no problem, we'll get it." He returned his eyes to Yates. "You think it's real? I always thought it was just a trick."

"We can't be certain the remedy will be a success, no. For this reason we've decided to include a not-withstanding clause in your contract, predicated upon the item's ability to function as speculated."

Steve narrowed his eyes. "A what kind of clause?"

Yates peeled back the skin of his briefcase and offered Steve a revised copy of our contract. To me he proffered a bulging manila envelope. I assumed it was filled with specs – photographs, information on the mark and his schedule, some aging magician badly in need of a haircut. "It's simple," Yates told us, referring to contracts, "if the item doesn't perform its intended purpose, you both agree to forfeit payment."

Steve flipped through the pages but it was clear he wasn't reading a word. "You never said anything about – "

"I believe our offer to retain your services is more than generous." Yates, employing all the languid force of his position, plucked the contract from between Steve's big fingers. After taking a moment to smooth the pages across the Graceland wet-bar, he produced an elegant ballpoint. "Please sign."

Steve glared, but after a moment he accepted the pen without saying anything. I did the same. Once the papers were autographed and copies scanned into Yates's handheld, we left Daniel Holloway to his untimely death.

Out in the corridor, Steve spat on the carpet. "Fucker," he commented, safely waiting until the door clicked quietly shut. "Tell me – just tell me that guy doesn't need his fucking teeth kicked in."

"We can't afford it."

Steve stared at the lock. "We can't afford it or *you* can't afford it?"

I coddled Steve with a sigh and tugged his sleeve toward the elevators. When Steve got angry he was a monster. Halfway down the hall, Steve shook free and followed me of his own accord. In any case, he was right. I couldn't afford to blow it.

There was a painting hung up between the elevators. A girl on a beach. She was standing up, her legs spread (but not too wide), looking out to sea. Both hands were up at her forehead, shielding her eyes from the sun, so the curve of her one visible breast was lifted, swept up by the tightness of skin. It looked to me like somebody's idea of a new life. It reminded me of Alice.

⊰(F)⊱

She was hiding behind one of the cracked-plastic menus, even though she knew all the dishes by heart. "I thought you might've stood me up."

"Never." I kissed her cheek. "Just busy with work." The waiter appeared and we both ordered spaghetti and a glass of water.

Without the menus between us, Alice leaned forward. "How'd the meeting go?"

"The what?"

"Your big meeting, remember?"

"Oh." I rubbed the bridge of my nose. "Yeah, it went well."

"Looks like it went miserably."

"Honestly, it went well. We got the job. First step, right? So now if

– well, we still have to, I guess close the sale. So the really big meeting is still coming." With Alice, nearly everything I did was a meeting. "But things look good."

"So more late nights?"

"One or two."

"But you're free on Tuesday, right?"

"Tuesday."

"I promised them three times already. You can't back out."

"Tuesday. Yeah, I think so."

Alice made an ugly face. She or I or both of us together had to work pretty hard to make Alice look ugly. "Dinner, remember? Dinner with my parents."

I laughed, a low, self-deprecating gurgle. "Shit. I'm sorry, I didn't forget. Tuesday night. No problem."

"Peter, listen, how do you think I feel? How do you think *they* feel? They're barely an hour out of the city and they've never met their soon-to-be son-in-law. It's ridiculous."

"I know. With my traveling and – but you're right. That's my fault. I've been too busy lately."

The waiter appeared with two plates of spaghetti and a plastic pitcher of well-iced tap water that smelled strongly of chlorine. We both let the food put a stall in the conversation. Alice laid a paper napkin across her thighs. It was hard to believe this place was her favorite restaurant; I'd convinced myself long ago she deserved better. "What do you think of Hawaii?"

Her attention stayed on her plate. "It's hot, it's beautiful. You know what I think of Hawaii."

"I know you always wanted to go, so why not on your honeymoon?"

That got her. All the ugliness was gone. "You're serious?"

I didn't answer right away. I puffed out my lip; I pretended to reconsider. "I don't know. I hear Jersey's nice."

"Peter!"

"Of course – yeah, I'm serious. I told you, the meeting went well and we got the job. So we're good as gold. Once I close the deal – " I reached across the table and covered her hand. "I love you, Alice." I said it again because I honestly meant it. "I love you."

She bit her lip. "Hawaii. I don't believe it." There was a conspiratorial gleam in her eye. It almost felt like we were planning a job together.

"Believe it. And I'm finally gonna meet your parents."

"Finally."

I twirled some spaghetti thoughtfully. "I just hope they like me."

"Me too. Maybe I should apologize in advance for my father."

I laughed. "Apologize? I haven't even met him yet. Give me some credit. He's gonna love me."

She slipped her other hand under mine; the little engagement ring scraped my palm. "Yeah, I'm just being silly."

◄(E)►

Steve had us booked into room 26 of a suitably anonymous place called Heaven's Oasis. Like a lot of motels, the name was inversely proportional to the quality of everything inside. The front doors were propped open with a rolled-up newspaper. A yellow sticky note was taped to the glass – PLEASE COME IN – but the front desk was abandoned. The stairwell smelled of mildew; the corridor smelled of urine.

Steve was waiting for me. When he opened the door he was just in his underwear, but he couldn't have been more imposing if he'd greeted me in a gorilla suit. In any case, he was almost as hairy. "What took you so long?"

"Dinner with Alice tonight. Afterwards we – you know."

"Fuck, Pete, you can't wait just a couple days? Until after the job?" Steve crossed the room to a pressboard table smeared with photographs of the magician's home. Some of the documents spilled over on the badly concaved bed. With a couple thick fingers, Steve pushed the photographs around the table. "You ever think that maybe people like you and me, people like us – shit, we never get *married*. Too much of a distraction."

"I think you take it too seriously."

"It is serious."

"Just a job. It's like any job."

"Says you."

"Says me."

Steve sighed. "What do you think about Tuesday?"

"For what?"

"For the job! The job like any job, you dumb shit."

I took a breath. "Why Tuesday? I think Tuesday's bad. I can't."

Steve hadn't yet looked up from the photographs. He laughed, mostly to himself. "What happened, you book a date?"

I didn't answer right away. Seeing him there – hunched over, dwarfing the table, the muscles in his back like a set of camel humps – it'd make anybody nervous. "Tuesday's bad."

"I guess you'll have to rearrange your schedule."

"I just can't."

Steve straightened up. "So what? Monday? *Sunday?* You wanna do it right now? Let's go."

"You know I need this to work out, so I don't want to screw it up. I want to plan it out. What about Wednesday, before sun-up?"

"Fuck, Pete." Steve pointed at the documents on the table. "His tour *ends* on Monday night, so already Tuesday cuts it pretty close. Wednesday's for shit."

"I just think it *has* to be Wednesday. I need that extra time. I need to practice."

Steve folded his arms over his chest; they hugged each other like a pair of hillsides. He uncoiled one and wagged a finger in my face. "What'd I tell you, Pete? We don't get married – it's not what we do." After that, he turned his back on me. He just stood there. I almost would've preferred a broken jaw.

"So what then? Wednesday's okay?"

He shook his head and pushed a puff of air out through his teeth. "Ever since we started together you've been wanting to 'start fresh', right? That's fine, and maybe this is it. But you ever think that maybe you first gotta *end fresh* before you start over again? You ever think of that?"

It was probably the wisest thing Steve had ever said to me, probably the smartest thing he'd said to anybody. I was flattered he said it to me. I stared at his back. The maze of tattoos that went across his shoulders and down his arms seemed oddly still; I was used to seeing them dance and swell as he moved. "So how about Wednesday," I asked, "before sun-up?"

Steve shrugged. "Fine. Wednesday."

I felt some of the tension run out of me and suddenly I remembered the six-pack I was carrying. I held it up. "You want a beer?"

Steve kept looking over the pictures. "Yeah, I do."

There was a bottle-opener screwed into the wall beside the light switch. I pried open two bottles and returned to the bed.

"Thanks."

I pointed at the photographs. "You think it'll work?"

"I fucking hope so."

"Me too. It's a lot of money."

Steve looked at me. "That's not what I meant. I told you about my cousin in Canada? Well she's sick, one of those new pneumonias. So if this thing works, then maybe – "

"Yeah, maybe. He's a magician right? So maybe."

We sat there for a while, looking over the specs on the mansion, the safe – what looked to be a standard Gardall – and all the drawings of the Box itself. We looked over everything and didn't say much. Not until the beers were finished. Steve handed me his empty. "Two more."

I was prying open the second bottle, with the first tucked under my elbow, when something went *snap* inside the bathroom. I flinched and the bottle under my arm slipped out and smashed to the floor. "Shit!" I looked behind me, through the half-shut bathroom door. "The fuck was that?"

Steve came over with a nasty grin on his face. He stepped over the splatter of glass and beer and switched on the bathroom light. "I hope that's *your* beer," he said, pointing at the floor. He crawled behind the toilet and when he stood up he was holding an enormous rattrap, complete with an enormous rat. It'd nearly been guillotined in two. Even still, it twitched furiously, each half trying vainly to escape. Steve held it up and blood poured into the sink, more than I would've expected. Steve held it up to his face and watched carefully until the rat went limp. "Yep," he said, "it's dead."

"Wonderful. So get rid of it."

With one hand, Steve snatched the un-smashed beer bottle from me. He took a long swallow and flicked the last of the rat's innards down the drain. "Whaddaya mean get rid of it? We need it."

"Ugh! What the hell for? Shit, we'll probably catch something."

"Shut up. Yates said the thing's gotta work, right? Well, this right here's our test case." Steve lowered the rattrap delicately, placing it in the sink as if was worth millions. And I realized yeah, maybe it was.

◁ **D** ▷

Alice's parents lived in a modest bungalow with pink aluminium siding. We turned into the driveway and I saw Alice's father for the first time

– standing in the garage, shirtless, coiling a black extension cord around his forearm. There was loose skin under his arms and more around his middle. He threw a dirty rag over his shoulder and came out into the sun, squinting.

"You must be Peter." He offered me his hand.

I took it and his name – I'd been repeating to myself the whole way there – crawled under one of the many rocks in my head. "Yeah," I said, "nice to finally meet you."

"Uh huh." He looked me in the eye. His grip didn't let up right away. "Gil. You can call me Gil."

"Right, of course. Wow. How are you?"

Alice stepped between us and slapped her father on his belly. "Honestly, Dad, you could've at least dressed yourself." Her father shrugged and pulled the rag off his shoulder. He wiped his hands and moved aside so Alice could lead us both indoors.

Alice's mother was dark and reedy. She reminded me of the worn wicker furniture we'd passed on the way in. Unlike Alice's father, however, her name was sitting right there, on the tip of my tongue. But I decided to be polite nevertheless. "Mrs Bremen," I said, "great to finally meet you."

"Please, Peter," she said, almost flirtatiously, "call me Heddy. Just a pity it took so long! Alice tells us you keep quite a busy schedule."

"Yeah, well, that's true I guess."

In the little dining room, Heddy had prepared an enormous dinner. There was Caesar salad with too much garlic; mashed potatoes with too much butter; vegetables fried up with too much heat. There was a whole roast chicken. Alice's father, covered up in a bleach-stained golf shirt, slapped me hard across the back. "What sort of man are you?"

"I'm sorry?"

He had two bottles under his arm. "Home-grown or limey?"

I never drink whiskey – not even with Steve – but I figured the bottle of JD was the wiser choice.

"Good man." He found us each a glass and poured generously.

During the meal, wherever I could, I steered conversation toward Alice – her childhood, her old friends, her old boyfriends. It wasn't just a diversion. It wasn't simply a façade to keep me from talking about 'work'. Alice's life, proudly recounted by her mother in liberal detail, was mesmerizing. The more harmless secrets that were brought to light, the more Alice's ears and throat blushed red and the more I wanted to hear.

Alice's father didn't offer much. In the time it took me to sip my way down to the bottom of the glass, he'd polished off the bottle. Eventually, after reluctantly cracking into the Glenlivet, he spoke up. "Peter," he said, gesturing at me with a carving knife, "Alice tells me you're in, what is it now, *speculation*?"

"Real estate. That's right."

"I hear you can make a bundle in that racket." He gouged the chicken and sliced away the last of the meat. "So that means what? You're rich?"

I gave everyone a weak smile. "Well, no, not rich. Not yet at least. It's like any investment, really." I was speaking by rote, recounting whatever I'd imagined myself saying to this man, from across this once-imaginary dinner table. "There's risk, certainly, but if things go well – and I'm anticipating they will, I mean with this next investment I'm involved in – then it's true, there's potential for a fairly large return."

Alice's father stared at the chicken on his plate. He gave a little nod.

I felt Alice's hand on top of mine. "The deal he's working on now," she chirped, "it's going to pay for the wedding."

Her father giggled and poked Alice's shoulder. "Just make sure you have him inspected beforehand."

"Gil!"

"What? I'm serious. Christ, everybody's got something these days."

Alice's mother gave me a bright smile. "I'm sure Peter is perfectly healthy." She shifted in her chair, turned her back on her husband. "From what Alice tells us, it certainly sounds like an exciting line of work. But now, when you say risk...?"

"Oh, nothing to worry about. In my line there's hardly any. I'm quite conservative really. One day, I'd love to let you see our office back east." I laughed like I believed it myself. "Honestly, we all look like a bunch of accountants."

Alice's father snorted.

"Dad!"

He raised his glass at me, practically in a toast. "I know about people, Alice." He looked at me. "We can smell our own, hey? I'd bet my ass that – well, let's just say you don't look like the accounting type to me. Hell, you don't even look like the *real estate* type." He exhaled. "Hnh. I don't know what you look like."

Heddy reached over the table. "Gil, really!"

"It's okay," I said. "I understand. I think I've always been a little rough around the edges." I looked Alice's father in his reddening eyes. I wondered if telling him my true vocation would be an easier pill for him to swallow. I imagined there was a good possibility that if I told him the truth – *Gil, your daughter's marrying a thief, and a damn good one* – he'd likely shake my hand and offer to rent the wedding hall. "With all due respect, sir, I've been a real-estate speculator all my professional life. I think it attracts people like me, because it can be so unpredictable. But that's exactly what I don't like. After I close this next deal, I'm hoping I'll be able to...settle down." I squeezed Alice's hand. The pressure shot up her arm and she grinned like a child.

Her father poured himself another glass. "Okay," he said, "so tell me about this project. I never thought *real estate* was such a big deal around here."

I pressed my lips together and took a breath. "Well, Mr Bremen, I only wish I *could* tell you. But the thing is my employers – the ones who retained my services in town – they don't want me discussing my work with anyone but them. Making a bid like this, it can be delicate sometimes. I'm sure you understand."

He frowned and climbed out his chair. "Mr Bremen – I already told you, call me Gil." He chewed the inside of his lip, picked up his glass and left the room.

"Dad?"

"Damn chairs're hell on my back," he said, "I'll be out here on the couch."

After a few minutes, we could hear him snoring.

◄(**C**)►

The safe was a problem. It was taking me longer than usual, longer than it ought to. It still looked like a standard Gardall, but the guy was a professional magician, so who knows – maybe there was nothing standard about it. Either that or else Steve was right, maybe Alice was a distraction. Behind me, he whispered, "Come on!" A pearl of sweat ran down the back of my arm and dropped off at the elbow. Something inside the Gardall clicked.

"Finally."

There was something inherently funny about cracking open a black box so you could liberate the Black Box inside. Ironically – or maybe not – the one inside looked even more secure than the one I'd just opened. It was made of heavy-gauge black iron, engraved with symbols that made me think of Steve's tattoos. Set in the lid was a tiny plasma view-screen and a few buttons, the only parts that didn't resemble a tiny treasure chest. Looking at it, I knew if it came with any sort of locking mechanism, it'd be nothing I could crack.

Steve put out his hands. "Lemme see."

"Careful. It's heavy as shit. You might as well carry it." I handed it to him and started rolling up my tools.

We were nearly out the door when the lights went on. Instinctively, we both ran. I'd left everything unlocked, just in case. But now, from the inside, the door was sealed tight.

"You'll find the entire building is closed. There's no way out."

We turned around and there was the magician, perched at the top of his awful gold-leaf staircase. His hair, dark red and grey, wafted up around his head like burning leaves. In his hand was a small gun, his other one balled up tight in the pocket of his housecoat.

I said, "We don't want any trouble."

The magician grinned. He came down a few more steps. "Neither do I. So put the Box on the floor and I'll open up the door. You'll be free to go."

Steve took a deep breath and pushed the device into my arms. "Here," he said, stepping forward, "lemme do my job." The second time I held it, the Box seemed even heavier.

Steve approached the staircase. He was looking at the gun. "I've been shot before," he said. "You don't wanna shoot me."

"You're probably right." The magician's fist came out of his pocket so casually I honestly thought he was offering to shake hands. But his hand was oddly sheathed in a white glove. He flicked his wrist and a fine powder settled over Steve's face. Initially, Steve barely flinched. And for a small instant I could see the magician was scared. But then Steve inhaled sharply, like a hiccup. Then he coughed. To his credit, he nearly made it to the bottom of the stairs. But then he fell forward, burying his face in his hands, sputtering like an old car.

The magician came down the remaining steps and joined us. "Your friend is stupid."

"What'd you do? What was that?" I crouched down by Steve and placed the Box on the floor beside him.

"It's not too much worse than mace. Not much."

Steve grunted. He was struggling to breathe.

"Of course," said the magician, stepping past us toward an archaic rotary-dial telephone that hung on the wall like a painting, "now I've no choice but to notify the police."

I stood up, wondering how to stop him. The gun was still there and it frightened me more than it'd frightened Steve. I caught myself thinking of Alice. "Listen," I said. Listen to what? What could I say that was worth listening to? "Keep the Box. We'll go."

The magician looked at me. The gun was levelled at my belly. He dialled with his gloved hand. I watched some of the powder sprinkle off his finger.

On the floor behind me, Steve screamed. I felt the muscles in my belly go tense and I assumed he was dying. But he wasn't. Instead, he was standing up. He was on his feet and he had the Box in both hands. It came down first on the magician's arm and then across his face. I knew enough to get down and when the gun fired, twice, the bullets missed us both. Somewhere nearby, I heard the shattering of glass.

When I looked back at the telephone, the magician was on the floor. Steve was pummelling him, mashing him with the Box. I tried pulling him back. "Steve, stop! Jesus!" He didn't stop right away. He took a few more swipes. When he did, I saw his face was like a balloon, raw and distended. He was wheezing. I'd never heard Steve wheeze before. He took a ragged breath and gave me the Box to carry. We escaped through a broken window.

◄ B ►

On our way back to Heaven's Oasis, we stopped at a drugstore. I told the pharmacist we'd been hiking. I told her Steve had fallen face-first into a bush of poison oak. Whether or not poison oak grew in bushes was a mystery to me. The pharmacist gave us a funny look, but did her job. She was helpful. She sold us a bottle of something dubiously called witch hazel, a tube of ointment, and a box of antihistamines. Steve's left eye had swollen entirely shut and he'd scratched the skin around his ear until it was bleeding.

Crouched in the aisle with the foot-remedies, I daubed Steve's face with the witch hazel and fashioned an eye-patch with tensor bandage. It was on the way out that we ran into Alice, standing at her car.

"Peter? Hi, how're – " She stopped because she saw Steve standing behind me, that we were a pair. "Are you okay? I thought you had an early meeting."

"I did – I mean we do. This is Steve. He's another agent with the firm. We work together sometimes. You won't believe what happened."

"Hi," said Steve, and offered Alice a little wave.

Alice came around her car and went straight for Steve, peering into his face. I hoped the huge discrepancy in their heights would soften her appraisal, but no. She took in a sharp breath and covered her mouth. "You need a hospital."

Steve sighed. "No. We still have to – " He looked at me stupidly. "Well, you know, we can't miss our next *meeting*, right?"

Alice laughed. It sounded nasty and unnatural. "You can't be serious. Look at you." She pointed. "That could be infected. You need a doctor."

Steve stood up straighter and winced with his one good eye. "I'm fine," he said, speaking through his teeth. He squeezed by her and out toward our rental. "C'mon, Pete," he said, without looking back, "let's get to that meeting."

Alice put her hand on my chest. "Peter. What's going on? Are you honestly trying to tell me that guy's a real estate agent?"

I looked past her, trying to see Steve as something he wasn't. "Oh, yeah, Steve's great. But no, you're right – he's in construction, actually. It's like I said, he's a contractor. We work together sometimes, two sides of the same coin. He builds it, I sell it."

"But you said – "

"I think he's upset after what happened. Oh, I never told you."

"Go ahead."

"He was mugged, Alice. Can you believe, it? Listen, I'll get him to a hospital. I promise."

"You promise."

I clicked my tongue. "Oh, now, c'mon. There's no need to look at me like that."

She lowered her voice. "Look at him. Who'd be dumb enough to mug somebody who looks like that?"

"Alice, you're being silly. It can happen to anyone." I pecked her cheek and with the slightest pressure, pushed her aside. "Anyway, you're right. I should get him to the hospital."

Alice looked at her hands. "I don't know, Peter. I've been thinking – "

I opened the driver's side door. "I promise. I'll get him to a hospital."

"Are you honestly in real estate? You can tell me."

I did my best to appear incredulous. "Alice, c'mon, that's your father talking. Of course I'm in real estate. Besides, what does he know? You said it yourself, he's a drunk." I dropped myself into the rental. I started the engine. Once we were paid, I thought, all'd be forgiven.

Alice stood on the curb. I could see her through the windscreen; she'd gone back to examining her hands. Her face was twisted up, but only a bit. It wasn't the ugly face she made when she got angry. But it wasn't her beautiful, regular face either. To be honest, I didn't know what it looked like, so I gave up trying to pin it down. I turned around in the seat, put the car in reverse.

◄(**A**)►

Steve shut the lid. The view-screen lit up red and green – readouts and figures that made little sense. The Box itself vibrated quietly. Steve tried clearing his throat again; he patted his face with the damp towel I'd given him. "What's it doing?" he asked, as if I knew. The shaking intensified and the screen came up with a simple sequence of letters. They appeared one at a time, backwards, beginning with G: G, G, G, G...F, F, F, F...E, E, E, E...

Steve coughed like somebody was choking him. "Letters," he growled, "G, F – whaddaya think they mean?"

I looked away from the Box and up at Steve's face. His other eye had swollen a bit, but it looked like he still had a pinprick to see through; the skin on his cheeks and forehead was still bright pink, but at least the blood on his neck had dried up. I didn't have an answer for him. "Jesus, Steve. Maybe you do need a hospital. Who knows what he sprayed you with, and there's some blood there so – what if you caught something? You could end up like Holloway."

Steve grimaced, conveyed the fact that I knew him better than that. "Alice isn't here, so shut up about the hospital. I'm not gonna end up like Holloway. If I did, what's the difference, now that we got our hands on this thing?"

The letters kept going, but they were slowing down. C...C...C...C... B...B...B...B... The thing was really shaking; the vibrations were so fierce

I thought the Box might flip off the table, maybe leap out the window. Then it went dead calm. The screen just said A. Nothing was flashing.

Steve looked at me. "It's finished."

"How do you know?"

"'A', right? That's the start. The thing works backward, right? That makes sense. So 'A' means it's done."

I threw up my hands. "You don't know that. How do you know that?"

"I'll tell you why – because while you were out with your lady friend half the time, I was stuck in here, and I actually read the specs." Steve opened up the Box. "Holy shit."

"What is it? It worked?"

Steve reached in. He took out the rat with his bare hands. The animal snuffled at the sharp black tattoos that went around his wrists. The rat looked at me. For whatever reason, I thought it looked hungry.

"You're fucking goddamn right it worked! And you can tell Alice the honeymoon's wherever the fuck she wants it. Shit, you can tell her she'll get ten honeymoons!"

Steve's enthusiasm was contagious. "Ten. Wouldn't be so bad."

"Here." Steve thrust the rat at me. But I refused to take it from him.

"I don't think we should touch it."

"Suit yourself." He put the thing down on the table and went for the phone that was bolted to the night stand. "I'm calling that skinny bastard – what's his name?"

"Yates. And remember you gotta dial nine." I looked down at the table and watched the rat skitter over the shitty pressboard. After only a few steps, the skittering turned to walking and then the walk degraded to a limp. After that, the rat stopped moving at all.

I heard Steve saying something into the phone, but I wasn't listening to the words. I leaned down, close to the table. I almost prodded the rat with my finger, but right in front of my eyes, its spine collapsed. Its head lolled to one side and a little bubble of blood popped from its mouth. The Box was a fraud. Just a trick.

I put myself between Steve and the table. I scooped up the rat. Its body was already ice-cold and stiff. I thought I could actually feel the thing rotting away, crumbling up in my hands. "Gotta take a leak," I said, over my shoulder, and I went to the bathroom.

I flushed the rat's body down the toilet and started scrubbing my hands with the motel's complimentary sliver of soap. I was still washing when Steve push open the door, beaming. "Yeah," he said, looking me dead in the eye, "so Holloway didn't make it, but everything's set up with Yates. Whenever we deliver the Box, it's pay day."

I raised my eyebrows. "Great."

"Where's the rat?"

I pointed at the open window. "I set him free."

Steve stared at the window for a moment. He clapped his huge, brotherly arm over my shoulders like a painted rug. "Christ, Pete – since when're you such a bleeding heart? No wonder you scored a girl like Alice."

"No wonder," I said.

THE GOLD WATCH

KEVIN PRUFER

The lady in the trunk would not wake up. The schoolboys jabbed her with a stick, shone their flashlights over her closed eyes, but she wouldn't stir. "Forget it," one of them said. Another agreed. "We already got the radio, what else do we need?" But when the third boy played his flashlight over the lady's still body, the glare caught on something shiny, something tempting. A delicate gold watch, a watch that looked like money, around her pale wrist. He leaned in, touched it gently, his finger sliding, for a moment, over the soft, cold skin just below her palm. The metal felt good against his fingers, cool and valuable, but the lady's arm was heavy, so it took him a moment to undo the clasp and, even then, it caught in her cool flesh, dragging a long scratch across her wrist before the watch came free. "Now we can go," he said.

The others looked at him curiously. "What you got?" they said. But before he could answer, a glare of headlights clicked on not fifty feet away, in the River Market lot. The lights blinded him and a car started up, pulled forward. The boy slid the watch quickly into his jacket pocket, then looked inside as the car eased silently beside him. Not a cop, but a man with a thin mustache was driving, a man who smiled at him, waved, something golden around his wrist, waved and pulled away.

Relieved, the boy felt the weight in his pocket, noticed the taillights now, watched the car until it disappeared onto James Street, and his friend said, "You sure that wasn't a cop?" But it wasn't, he knew. He'd seen the face before, but where?

So they walked down Compton Avenue toward Vine Street, and the boy kept thinking about the lady's wrist, the thin green veins beneath the skin – had he seen them, or was he creating them now, in his head? – the cold skin and how her arm, when he tried to remove the watch, wouldn't give, but cracked almost imperceptibly. How long had she been asleep? he thought, because he didn't want to think she was dead, that he'd taken the watch from a dead person. How long until the arms grow stiff and cold? The watch in his jacket pocket felt heavy and when he touched it, too cold, and he found to his surprise that he didn't really want it anymore, he didn't want it, but what could he do? He'd have to hold onto it, and his two friends, laughing and talking about the stiff, the dead bitch in the trunk, well, he didn't feel like laughing.

When they got to 27th street, he said he thought he'd crash out for the night, he was getting a cold, and they laughed at that. "What you gonna do with that watch, dog?" one of them asked, and the boy smiled and said he'd probably sell it, you know, they'd all see their share. And the other two laughed, said, "You better, boy, we'll come asking," and they continued down the dark street until they disappeared.

But the third boy didn't go to bed. Instead he walked to the pay phone, dropped in a couple coins, and dialed. The air was getting cold and felt like October and he shivered in his thin jacket. "There's a lady," he told the operator who answered, "a lady and she's not moving or nothing, she's not moving, but I seen her in the trunk of this car."

Armand leaned over the trunk while Franklin set up the spotlight, adjusted it so it shone neatly over the woman's body. She seemed at peace in the square glow, her knees folded neatly, her head aslant, lips parted, cracked, and dry. The uniform who'd responded to the 911 did his job well. He hadn't touched a thing, had radioed dispatch, which sent the message off to homicide. The night desk there had called Armand at home, where he sat in front of the television, well into his third bourbon and lime. "Dammit," he'd said, "can't you get Fitzwilliams? Can't you get Johnson?" but the desk said no, said Armand was on call, so he stubbed his cigarette out in the last of his drink, turned off the set, and put on his jacket. He'd forgotten it was his night, so he ate six or seven Certs on the way to the scene, hoping Franklin wouldn't smell the bourbon on his breath, though he always did. And sure enough Franklin raised his eyebrows and smiled at him, said, "Long night already, huh?" then adjusted the spotlight and taped down the crime scene.

Franklin acted like that sometimes, like Armand hadn't done a worth-while thing in five years, not since his wife and son died. But it wasn't true, he'd been a good cop. And evenings were hardest, alone at home. "Did you see the stiff's arm?" Franklin asked, after a painful minute, rolling fresh film into his camera.

"What about it?"

"No bracelet, no watch, no jewelry at all."

Armand nodded. He'd noticed. The Charm Killer always left something around the wrist, so this was something new. A change in the M.O.?

Armand looked more closely at the dead woman's arm. It wasn't right. It rested in a way that wasn't, well, natural. Armand couldn't explain it. He snapped on a pair of surgical gloves, then lifted the arm, which rose way too easily, and took a closer look. Yes, something wrong, something wrong. A long scratch on the wrist that never bled. He touched it gently with his gloved hand, ran his finger over it. It should have bled, but it hadn't. "No bracelet, no watch," Armand said into the trunk, "but she had one. Someone ripped it off of her, post mortem." He lowered her arm again, then looked around the edge of the car to where Franklin snapped one photo after another of the wheel wells, the windshield.

When Downtown called his cell and told him that the car belonged to a woman last seen in Westport, he wasn't surprised. The Charm Killer sometimes hunted there, among the wine bars and coffee houses, the art theatre and sushi joints, the places where KC's young and free congregated beneath phony old-style lampposts or in dark, comfortable bars drinking imported beers and talking about the latest foreign films. Normally, he had no time for Westport, though years ago – before the car accident, before his wife and son died – a long, long time ago, he was one of them, young, outspoken and careless. Now he drank at home.

The schoolboy, Lamar, turned the watch over and over in his hands. It felt heavier than he thought it should, and the second hand swept evenly and fluidly across the face. He frowned and put it to his ear, but he couldn't hear it ticking, just a low hum that said money, money, money. He didn't like it. It was a cursed thing, and he thought about throwing it in the wastebasket or down the incinerator chute outside his mom's apartment door, but he couldn't. It was too beautiful, too perfect, the most perfect thing he'd ever held.

But what of the back of the watch, the engraving? FOR J.L., MY LITTLE BIRD. TONY BOY. What did it mean? He closed his eyes, but when he did, he saw the lady's thin, white neck, her wrist, the green veins beneath the soft skin, the watch, how it glittered in the flashlight's glow. No, no, he thought. Stop it. And he put the watch carefully on the floor beside his bed and turned out the light.

When he closed his eyes, he remembered the white face in the big car, the hand that waved – he'd seen that man before, hadn't he? Somewhere? – the car going past and past him, again and again. But when he dreamed, it was the watch he saw glowing, the dull hum the gears made, the second hand sweeping smoothly around and around. He dreamed about the sleeping lady's eyes, half shut, eyelids quivering like bird's wings, what they'd look like open, cold and blank.

The Charm Killer liked gold, but he never kept it long. Armand knew that for sure. The killer liked gold and maybe he hung around the wine bars and bookshops in old Westport, found his marks there, charmed them – how did he do it? – got into their cars with them and drove through the night, downtown past Union Station, past the war memorial and the hulking Kemper Arena toward River Market, where he shot them once in the head and stuffed them in their own trunks. Sometime, maybe before he killed them, maybe after, he slipped something gold around their wrists, something he'd stolen from his previous victim. Always he stole from one victim to give to the next. That's why they called him the Charm Killer. That and he must be a pretty charming guy, Armand figured.

So Armand knew exactly what he was looking for. An old gold watch – a 1967 Elgin, to be exact – with an engraving: FOR J.L, MY LITTLE BIRD. TONY BOY. It belonged to the body they'd found last month – Jennifer Lagaurdia, the sixth victim – outside the old dry goods building.

But what had the killer taken from this new body? What was Kitty Dufresne missing? Her boyfriend, a lawyer with Hallmark, suggested it might have been a gold bracelet from which hung fifteen or twenty little gold coins. "She got it," he said, "in Morocco. The little coins, she loved them, the noise they made." At the time, Armand nodded sympathetically. He knew he'd see it soon enough, on another victim's wrist.

He and Franklin were driving up Broadway now, past the ragged warehouses and the restored ones. Every month, another warehouse opened its doors to gentrification, another health food store, another coffee shop. "Damn yuppies," he said. Franklin laughed. He wanted a drink.

"You know," Franklin had said earlier that day, "I bet you anything the kid who called in the 911 stole it."

"From the scratch," Armand had said, "I'd say he was in a hurry."

They'd driven all day, checking leads, waiting for Downtown to call with something on the 911, where it had come from. And when Downtown did call, finally, Armand held the cell phone to his ear, driving one-handed. The 911, Downtown said, came in from the projects on 27th and Broadway, the pay phone outside the 2705 building, so Armand turned the unmarked cruiser around and parked on 26th.

He'd listened to the 911 a few times already and thought he had a good sense of the voice – "a lady and she's not moving or nothing" – it sounded like a boy's, maybe twelve, thirteen. Black. Scared. He tried to remember it, until Franklin said, "We gonna be obvious out here, man. They can smell a cop," and Armand said nothing in response, because of course it was true.

"Hey," Franklin said, "You hear? We just gonna go right in?"

Armand smiled and kept walking.

"Oh, hell," Franklin said. "All this because the girl got a scratch on her wrist? Ten bucks says the kid doesn't give up the watch."

They spent a couple hours going door to door through 2705 without any luck. An old lady told them there were several boys between ten and fifteen in the building. "They're good kids," she said. "Most of them."

In the courtyard across the street, a group of them leaned against a chain link fence and laughed. The wind blew in from downtown and they had their windbreakers wrapped around them tight. Franklin smiled. "We're looking to buy a watch," he said. "Any of you boys know where we could buy a real nice gold watch?"

The boys looked away or at their feet. One smiled toothily, hands in pockets. Trouble, Armand thought, but the boy just laughed, said, "Whatchoo want a watch for? Try J.C. Penney's, dog." And the others laughed and kicked the dirt with their sneakers.

The sun was going down. Franklin smiled. "Tried that," he said. "They don't have what I want. I'm looking for something particular." The boys were still laughing at the crack about Penney's. "I'm looking for something gold and square, got writing on the back. I'll pay fifty bucks better than pawn."

The boys just laughed. "Damn," the oldest said, "damn, Mr Money, fuck you."

So Armand took out a handful of his cards, dropped them carelessly in the dirt. "If anyone knows where my friend can buy a watch like this," he said. "Gimme a call. It's his birthday coming up. I want to get him something nice."

And they walked away.

Lamar lay on the torn yellow sofa, the watch humming on the cushion beside him. Funny, he thought, how it hums and doesn't tick. When he closed his eyes, he still saw the dead lady – he could say it now, the dead lady, the dead lady – he still saw her blank face, her wrists. He remembered unclasping the watch, how it caught in her flesh as he pulled it away. It was a beautiful watch, but cursed.

He lay on the sofa and watched the muted TV, listened to the noises of the neighborhood, the honking horns, the kids still up and laughing in the courtyard. The watch just hummed. The television's blue light flickered over his face. He held Armand's card in his hand, turned it over and over. "Thug," his friends told him, "sell that! They ain't gonna do nothing. You didn't kill no one. You just found a watch. 5-o don't care about you. Sell that!"

He picked up the watch, weighed it in his hand, looked at the card, then rose from sofa and walked into the kitchen. There was no one home – his father long gone and away, his mother working – so he picked up the phone and dialed.

"You did the right thing," Armand said. Lamar sat in the seat beside him, where he'd feel important. Franklin was somewhere else, city hall, running down leads.

"I didn't kill no girl," Lamar said. "She was dead. I just took the watch."

"It's fine," Armand said. "It's fine." He liked the boy. He was a thoughtful kid, smart. "I know you didn't kill anyone. What I want to know is, did you see anyone?"

They were driving toward the precinct station and the boy seemed lost in thought. "Yeah," he said at last. "I seen someone, but I didn't kill no one."

"Who did you see?"

"I dunno," the boy said. He looked out the window, at the warehouses. "Just someone."

"Near the body?" Armand asked. He tried to sound casual, nonchalant, but it didn't come off right.

The boy was silent.

"Near the body?"

"Not near the body," the boy said, at last. "In this car, see? This car pulls out of nowhere and we figured it was 5-0, but, you know. It slows and I seen inside."

Armand waited for more.

"And this white guy, he's waving at me, like hello." Lamar laughed, but not nicely. "He's like, hello, kid, hello, friend."

Armand nodded. "Would you recognize him if I showed you a few pictures?"

The boy shrugged. Like, how should he know? And when he did that, Armand remembered his own son. Five years later, and he still missed him, his laugh, even his insolence. The last time he'd seen him, they'd argued and argued, he and his 10-year-old son, his wife, and then she'd driven him away, away up the snowy highway toward Maryville and he never saw them again.

"You all right?" the boy said beside him. "You always quiet like that?"

"I want you to try to remember that man's face," Armand said.

Lamar didn't know, he didn't know. He'd lain awake two nights remembering the car ease past, the cold, white face peering at him, the hand that waved. Did he have a moustache? Lamar thought so. Was his face narrow or wide? Narrow, it seemed, but maybe not. He knew well enough that when he recalled a thing, it changed. It changed with every recollection, mutated, became, always, another thing. A thing remembered enough never bore much resemblance to the thing itself, so Lamar had no faith in his own recollections. It was a white man, certainly, and he thought the man had a moustache, but beyond that? The bit of gold around his wrist – that was certainly a true memory, it was so odd. The man had worn a bracelet that shone when he waved.

"Yeah," he said as Armand turned the pages in the binder. Lamar examined face after face. "I don't know," he said. "It was only a second."

"Just relax, relax," Armand said. "Relax and look at them and tell me if anything jumps out at you."

Lamar turned a few more pages, but his eyes wouldn't focus. "I can't remember," the boy said. He couldn't relax. He couldn't relax, he wanted to do things right, but he couldn't relax. He tried to conjure up the image of the man in the car, but all he could think of was the dead lady, her knees pulled up to her chest, her arm, the watch. He wished he hadn't taken it. He wished they hadn't gone anywhere near that car, near Kitty Dufresne's car. "I can't remember," he said, and he was crying now. "Damn," he said, "it was hectic, and I can't – "

Armand closed the book. "It's all right," he said. He patted the kid on the hand. "It's all right," but the kid was crying now, long tears streaming down his face. "It's all right," Armand said. "You did your best."

But the kid wouldn't stop crying, and Armand walked him outside to the lobby where his mother was supposed to be waiting – they'd called her, she'd come in from work and had been in the lobby when the two of them had gone into the interview room to look at the books – but she wasn't there.

"Where's his mom?" Armand asked Ginny, who was sitting behind the desk.

"She left," Ginny said.

"She left?"

"She left. Said you should give the kid a ride home. She had to get to work."

Lamar sniffed beside him. "What the fuck?" Armand said. "She just left?"

Ginny shrugged.

Armand looked down at Lamar. The kid was big for his age – a little pudgy, a big navy blue windbreaker on – and still crying a little. "I guess I'm taking you home," he said.

So, they drove downtown. "Your mother just leave you places like that a lot?"

"You know," the kid said, "hectic life." He wasn't crying anymore, had regained a little of his swagger.

"Must be," Armand said. "What does she do that's so important?"

The kid shrugged.

"You don't know?"

"She works, you know, here and there. Down at Cloud 9. At Fantasies. Wherever."

Armand nodded. He knew what that meant. "You see her much?"

"Days," Lamar said. "When I'm not in school."

They pulled in front of 2705 Broadway. "Keep going," Lamar said. "Drop me by Myron's Deli, up there on 23rd. I'll walk."

Armand nodded. The kid didn't want his friends to see him, wanted to keep the $80 for the watch, maybe. He pulled a few blocks further, dropped the kid by the Deli, watched him disappear inside.

It was hot there. A group of boys Lamar didn't know were playing pinball, jamming their hips against the machine, laughing. Damn, dog, damn! You gotta smack that fucker or he'll go right down the hole. Shut up, bitch.

Lamar looked around. He only meant to disappear into the Deli and get his bearings, to check things out, then walk away casually, down the street like he'd just come from playing pinball, from buying a pack of cigs and was on his way home, But now he was hungry and he had a wad of cash – $80 – the cop had given him for the watch, and the potato chips looked good. He picked out a bag of Lays Bar-B-Q, wandered over to the pinball machine where the older boys were, watched them a little bit. He'd never played, and the little silver ball fascinated him, bouncing back and forth, clanging and ringing off the paddles.

After a few minutes, he made his way to the register, where a white guy took his money and smiled. Myron, he thought, but the guy was too young, maybe twenty-five or thirty, and he knew the Deli had been on this corner forever. New guy, probably. Lamar had seen him once or twice. When the guy smiled, he noted a gold front tooth. Slick, he thought. He wanted one like that.

That night, he slept in his jeans and T-shirt. His pajamas were in the wash and his mother was out, wherever she went. So what? he thought, so what? He had a roll of cash and he'd sleep in whatever he wanted to.

But when he closed his eyes, he kept seeing the woman's body, and the headlights, the car sliding past while the man inside waved at him, the bit of gold around his wrist. Lamar knew about the Charm Killer – he wasn't stupid – and he knew, now, what that gold might be. Another watch, a bracelet, something the killer stole. He'd figured it out at the police station. The watch Lamar had stolen belonged to some other dead lady.

He tried to sleep. He tried and tried, his eyes squeezed shut. He counted his breaths, then tried to breathe slower. He counted the headlights that slid past his window, illuminating the cracked walls, the water-stained ceiling. No good, no good. He kept seeing the green veins in the wrist, the eyes, rolled back and blank, the car.

He thought about his mother – where was she? – and his father, long gone. He thought about Armand, who was 5-o, but he liked him. Armand seemed sad and quiet and not like a cop at all. When Armand patted him on the head, it was like his own father might have, the way he imagined his own father would be. Lamar thought about that, and the wind whispered past the house, and the boys in the courtyard cried out and laughed in the night, and then he was asleep, he was asleep.

And in his dream, the car pulled past again, and the white guy leaned forward and smiled, he waved and smiled, the car humming past – humming like the watch hummed, finely tuned, a nice car – the car hummed past and the man smiled. He smiled and his smile was like a gash, and, in his dream, Lamar looked at him and when the man waved, Lamar felt the watch in his pocket. Such a nice watch, so expensive and deadly. And the man waved and smiled and there was gold around his wrist. He smiled, and then Lamar saw it, a flash of gold in his smile, a wink of gold, a gold tooth. The man smiled and his front tooth was gold and, seeing that, Lamar woke up. He was sweating, The room was silent. It was almost morning.

"How'd you get here?" Armand said. "Aren't you supposed to be in school?" But, secretly, Armand was glad to see the boy. He liked him.

"The man," Lamar said, "I think I seen him yesterday."

"In the book?"

Lamar shook his head. "In real life. I seen him at this Deli, see?"

"You sure?"

Lamar thought about that. Was he? "I don't know," he said. "Sometimes I think about something a long time, and then it's like it's true. I don't know."

"But you think – "

"I think. I think I seen him. I think I seen his gold tooth when he passed that night, and then I seen it again."

"What Deli?" Armand was putting on his raincoat. It was raining out and Lamar was dripping wet. He tossed the kid his only umbrella, then walked with him from his office past the front desk and the waiting room, down the hall and into the garage, where they got in the unmarked Chevy Impala.

"This Deli," Lamar was saying. "Myron's Deli. You know, where the high school kids hang out. I seen him there. He's been there for a couple weeks, because I seen him before I took the watch. I just didn't remember."

"He's a high school kid?" Armand sounded doubtful.

"No. He's the guy working the counter. Making the sandwiches. I seen him before and I almost recognized him that night, but I didn't."

"You tell anyone else?" Armand asked. They were pulling to the side of the road now. "Your mother, your friends, anyone?"

"Ain't seen my mother since day before yesterday," the boy said. "Ain't told a soul."

"And did the guy seem to recognize you? The guy with the gold tooth?"

The kid shrugged. "I dunno," he said. "Maybe."

When they got out of the car, it was raining even harder than before, so Armand pulled the hood of his raincoat over his head and jogged into the store, Lamar right behind him. Myron's was crowded again, the same group of high school kids playing pinball, banging the edge of the machine with their hips, laughing. One of them put a quarter on the glass, called next game.

"Be cool," Armand told Lamar, taking off his jacket, tucking it under his arm. "I'm gonna order a couple of sandwiches and when you see the guy, hold your horses until we sit down."

But this time, it wasn't a guy at the register, but a young, dark-haired woman, maybe nineteen or twenty, exotic, maybe Arab or Italian. When she smiled, Armand noticed her nice teeth, and he ordered a couple pastramis on rye with relish and mustard. She rang those up, and he added a couple Cokes, glancing over her shoulder toward the kitchen, where two black guys were making sandwiches. A fat old man with a moustache – probably Myron, maybe the girl's father – sat at a table in the corner with a pile of receipts and the boys at the pinball machine shouted and laughed. He felt Lamar breathing beside him.

"You all right?" the girl said.

Armand nodded. He was fine. He gave Lamar one of the Cokes, told him to go sit down.

"Twelve fifty-five," she said.

And Armand pulled out his wallet and gave her a twenty, trying to get a better look into the kitchen to see if someone else was in there, around the corner, or working the microwave. But he couldn't see and the girl counted out the change and handed it to him, a pile of ones and some coins clattering into his palm.

But the clattering didn't sound quite right, and he looked down just as the girl was pulling back her palm. Around her wrist was a gold bracelet with maybe twenty tiny gold coins jangling from little chains.

Somehow, Myron's Deli got very quiet just then. The coins gleamed on top of the bills in his hand and Armand looked at the bracelet around the girl's wrist, at the little gold coins dangling from it. Rain tapped against the windows. And then the noise in the Deli resumed.

"You sure you're all right?" the girl asked. "Sir?" she said, glancing nervously toward Myron, who hadn't noticed.

Armand opened his wallet and slid the bills inside, then turned it so she could see his badge. "Don't say anything," he said. Then, "Now, quietly, tell me where you got that bracelet."

"Jimmy gave it to me," she said. The door opened and a couple more kids came in. They skulked over to the cooler, reached in, pulled out a couple popsicles. It was raining even harder outside, rain filling the streets and sluicing over the great Deli windows.

"Jimmy work here?" Armand asked, as casually as he could.

"Used to," she said. "He quit. Just yesterday. What's this about?" She glanced over to Myron again, but he was busy with the receipts.

"He got a gold tooth?" Armand asked. "Good looking guy with a gold tooth?"

"Yeah," she said. "Is he in trouble?"

"I want to talk to him," Armand said. "That's all. You know where I can find him?"

She shrugged. "I'm seeing him tonight," she said. "We're going out. I'm supposed to pick him up, you know? At 9pm. His car's broke."

"Where you picking him up?" he asked.

"Westport," the girl said. "He's not in some kind of trouble, right? Because if he is, I hardly know him. He just gave the bracelet to me yesterday, when he asked me out." The boys were waiting behind Armand now, holding their popsicles. Armand stepped aside so they could pay.

Lamar was sitting at the table by himself. He was looking at Armand, his eyebrows raised, an unopened Coke in his hands. He turned back to face the girl at the counter.

"He said it would look good on me, he said I should wear it on our date." She shrugged. "It's stolen, right? I knew there was something funny about him." She had big, innocent eyes and Armand liked that. But he nodded.

"I'm going to need to talk to you," Armand said. "Before you go to meet him. I'll be sitting right there – " he gestured with his head toward the table toward Lamar. "I don't want you getting in trouble with Myron, but when you get a break, come sit down with us."

The sad thing was, she did look good in that bracelet. It suited her perfectly – jangly, eastern. It was just right for a young, exotic girl with long, curly black hair and olive skin, and Armand could see why the Charm Killer – why Jimmy – had chosen her. But he wouldn't get her. He wouldn't get her, because Armand was going to call Franklin at the station, and Franklin would talk to Bowery, and Bowery would talk to the Chief, and they'd set something up. It was as good as done.

He sat at the table with Lamar. The sandwiches arrived and they began to eat. The girl behind the counter kept looking at him, concerned.

She had a right to be worried, but it would go down just fine. They'd have a couple street cops in plainclothes on the sidewalk in Westport by 6pm, even in the rain, and they'd have a car at each corner. And Armand would ride with the young woman in her Honda to the meeting point, he'd ride with her and, when they got there, she'd point the guy out and Armand would call it in. "The guy in the black coat, corner of New Hampshire and 41st," he'd say. And wouldn't that guy be surprised then, when the radio cars pulled up in the rain, their lights flashing? Wouldn't he be surprised, surrounded on the street corner in Westport, the cars flashing lights in the rain and nowhere for him to go, nowhere at all?

Armand thought about how it would feel when he snapped the cuffs on the Charm Killer. Nice silver cuffs for the Charm Killer's wrists. A satisfying click, and his partner, Franklin, coming around the corner, gun drawn, serious, as ever. Armand hadn't felt this strong in a long time, the Charm Killer lying on the sidewalk in the rain, cuffed, his jacket and hair grown wet, his gold tooth glinting in the street lamp's glare.

The girl behind the register was coming on break now, hanging up her apron, coming around the counter to meet them. Armand gave her his most casual smile, then looked across the table at Lamar, who was just finishing his sandwich. "I think you did good," he told the boy. "You did real good, kid."

Lamar smiled, sipped his Coke. The rain beat down on the windows. For a second, Armand remembered his own son, but he pushed that away. The kid kept smiling.

"Anyone ever tell you that before, Lamar? You did damn good." ✺

WORK IN PROGRESS

SCOTT NICHOLSON

The cutting was the most demanding.

During his career as an artist, John Manning had sliced glass, trimmed paper, chipped granite, chiseled wood, shaved ice, and torched steel. Those materials were nothing compared to flesh. Flesh didn't always behave beneath the tool.

And bone might as well have been marble, for all its delicacy and stubbornness. Bone refused shaping. Bone wanted to splinter and curl, no matter how light John's touch on the hammer.

How did you build yourself alive?

Bit by bit.

Karen on the wall was a testament to that. Because Karen never lied.

And was never finished, an endless work in progress.

So building himself had become a mission from God. John knew from his time at college that art required suffering. He'd suffered plenty, from no job to canceled grants to broken fingers to Karen's last letter. His art had not improved, though he'd faithfully moved among the various media until his studio was as cluttered as a crow's nest.

He crushed out his cigarette and studied the portrait. Much of it had been done from memory. The painting had grown so large and oppressive in his mind that it assumed capital letters and became The Painting.

When he'd started it three years ago, the memory had flesh and was in the same room with him. Now he had to stagger through the caves of his brain to find her and demand she undress and model. And she had been so elusive lately.

Karen.

Her letter lay in a slot of his sorting shelf, just above a cluster of glass grapes. The paper had gone yellow, and rock dust was thick across its surface. If he opened the letter and read it, maybe she would come out of the smoky caves inside his skull. Except then he'd have to finish The Painting.

Looking out the window was easier, and had a shorter clean-up period. Painting had been foolish anyway. Every stroke was wrong. When he needed a light touch, he cut a fat swath. When he needed bold colors, he bled to mud.

He was born to sculpt, anyway. And now that he had the perfect subject, his frustrations could fall away. The anger and passion and sickness and hatred could go into the new work in progress and not poison his brain any longer. No more dallying with oil and charcoal, no more dancing with acrylics. That was a dilettante's daydream, and the dream was over.

Because this was real.

This was the most important moment in the history of art.

This was The Living Painting.

Except the materials didn't cooperate. Not Cynthia nor Anna and not Sharon in the trunk of his Toyota.

Life was a work in progress. Nothing was sacred. Art was a work in progress. Nothing was sacred.

If you rearranged the letters of *sacred*, you got *scared*.

John had not been scared when he asked Cynthia to be his material. Cynthia was a work in progress. Cynthia was an artist. Cynthia was art.

The body beneath the canvas in the corner of John's studio dripped.

John wondered if the blood would seep between the cracks in the floor and then through the ceiling of the used bookstore below. Even if it did, no one would notice for months. His studio was above the Classics, a section almost as long-dead as the authors themselves. Proof that even when you created something for the ages, the ages could care less.

So all that was left was pleasing himself. Envisioning perfection, and striving for it. Pushing his hands and heart to match his mind's strange hope.

He lifted the razor and was about to absolve himself of failure forever when the knock came at the door.

The studio was a shared space. John loathed other human beings, and other artists in particular, but his lack of steady income had forced him to join five others in renting the makeshift gallery. They were drawn together by the same fatalistic certainty of all other dying breeds.

Knock, knock.

And the knock came again. Some people didn't take no answer for an answer.

One of the five must have knocked. Probably wanted to chat about art. Not like they had anything better to do. John threw a spattered sheet of canvas over the corner of the room and went to the door.

Karen.

Karen in the hallway, glorious, almost perfect.

The last person he expected to see, yet the right person at this stage of the work in progress.

Karen as a statue, as a painting, as the person who shaped John's life. John tried to breathe but his lungs were basalt. Karen had not aged a bit. If anything, she had grown younger, more heavenly. More perfect.

John could read her eyes as if they were mirrors. She tried not to show it, but truth and beauty couldn't lie. Truth and beauty showed disapproval. That was one look she hadn't forgotten.

John weighed every ounce of the gray that touched his temples, measured the bags under his eyes, counted the scars on his hands.

"Hello John," Karen said.

Just the way she'd started the letter.

"Hi." His tongue felt like mahogany.

"You're surprised." Karen talked too fast. "My old roommate from college still lives here. I had her look you up."

"And you came all this way to see me?" John wanted a cigarette. His hands needed something to do.

"I was passing through anyway. Mountain vacation. You know, fresh air and scenic beauty and all that."

John glanced out the window. A plume of diesel exhaust drifted through his brick scenery. College buildings sprawled against the hillsides in the background. The mountains were lost to pollution.

John had been silent too long and was about to say something, but his words disappeared in the smoky caves inside his head.

"I'm not interrupting anything, am I?" Karen asked.

"You're not interrupting. I was just thinking about my next piece."

That meant his next sculpture rather than his next sexual encounter. Karen knew him well enough to understand.

She could never interrupt, anyway. John was an artist, and artists never had anything to interrupt. Artists had years of free time, and artists would rather give their free time to other people. Art was sacrifice.

His time was her time. Always had been. At least, it had been years ago. Now she lived two thousand miles away with no forwarding address and John had endless buckets of time to devote to his art.

Except now she stood at the door of his studio, eyes like nickels.

"Can I come in, then?"

Come.

In.

To John's studio.

With Cynthia lying in the corner, weeping blood and becoming. Becoming what, John wasn't sure.

Himself, maybe. His soul. The shape of things. A work in progress.

John tried on a smile that felt fixed in plaster. "Come in."

Karen walked past him and lifted objects from his workbench. "A metal dolphin. I like that."

She touched the stone sailboat and the driftwood duck and the rattlesnake walking stick and John watched her until she finally saw the portrait.

Or rather, The Painting.

"Damn, John."

"I haven't finished it yet."

"I think you just liked making me get naked. You painted me slow."

Not as slow as he should have. He wanted the painting to take a lifetime. She had other plans, though she hadn't known it at the time.

"It's a work in progress," he said.

"What smells so funny?"

Oh, God. She had flared her wondrous nostrils. John did not like where this was headed.

"Probably the kerosene," John said. "Cheaper than paint thinner, and works just as well, if you overlook the stink."

"I remember."

She remembered. She hadn't changed.

Had John changed?

No, not *Had John changed?*. The real question was how *much* John had changed. A soft foam pillow in the corner was studded with steak knives.

"Did you ever make enough money to buy an acetylene torch?" She ran a finger over the rusted edge of some unnamed and unfinished piece. "I know that was a goal of yours. To sell enough stuff to – "

John knew this part by heart. "To buy an acetylene torch and make twelve in a series and put an outrageous price on them, hell, add an extra zero on the end and see what happens, and then the critics eat it up and another commission and, bam, I'm buying food and I have a ticket to the top and we have a future."

Karen ignored that word *future*. She was the big future girl, the one with concrete plans instead of sandstone dreams. John's future was a dark search for something that could never exist. Perfection.

Karen walked to the corner, hovered over the spattered canvas.

No one could see it until he was finished.

John looked at the shelf, saw a semi-carved wooden turtle. He grabbed it and clutched it like a talisman. "Hey. I'll bet you can't guess what this is."

Her attention left the mound beneath the canvas. "How could I ever guess? You've only made five thousand things that could fit in the palms of your hands."

"Summer. That creek down by the meadow. The red clover was fat and sweet and the mountains were like pieces of carved rock on the horizon. The sky was two-dimensional."

"I remember." She turned her face away. Something about her eyes. Were they moist? Moister than when he'd opened the door?

She went to the little closet. John looked at her feet. She wore loafers; smart, comfortable shoes. Not much heel.

Beneath the loafers rested Anna. The experiment.

The smell had become pretty strong, so John had sealed the area with polyurethane. The floor glowed beneath Karen's shoes. John let his eyes travel up as far as her calves, then he forced his gaze to The Painting.

"Aren't you going to ask me about Hank?" she said.

As if there was any possible reason to ask about Hank. Hank had been Henry, a rich boy who shortened his name so the whiz kids could relate. Hank who had a ladder to climb, with only one possible direction. To the top where the money was.

Hank who could only get his head in the clouds by climbing. Hank who didn't dream. Hank who was practical. Hank who offered security and a tomorrow that wasn't tied to a series of twelve metal works with an abstract price tag.

"What about Hank?" he heard himself saying.

"Ran off." She touched a dangerous stack of picture frames. "With an airline attendant. He decided to swing both ways, a double member in the Mile High club."

"Not Hank?" John had always wondered about Hank, could picture him reverting to Henry and going to strange bars. Hank had been plenty man enough for Karen, though. Much more man than John.

At least the old John. The new John, the one he was building, was a different story.

A work in progress.

"What are you doing here?" he asked.

She turned and tried on that old look, the one that worked magic four years ago. Four years was a long time. A small crease marred one of her perfect cheeks.

"I came to see you," she said. "Why else?"

"Oh. I thought you might have wanted to see my art."

"Same difference, silly."

Same difference. A Karenism. One of those he had loathed. And calling him *silly* when he was probably the least silly man in the history of the human race. As far as serious artists went, anyway.

"No, really. What are you doing here?"

"I told you, Hank's gone."

"What does that have to do with me?"

She picked up a chisel. It was chipped, like his front tooth. She tapped it against a cinder block. Never any respect for tools.

"It has everything to do with you," she said.

A pause filled the studio like mustard gas, then she added, "With us."

Us. Us had lasted seven months, four days, three hours, and twenty-three minutes, give or take a few seconds. But who was counting?

"I don't understand," he said. He had never been able to lie to her.

"You said if it wasn't for Hank – "

"Henry. Let's call him Henry."

Her eyes became slits, then they flicked to the Andy Warhol poster. "Okay. If it wasn't for Henry, I'd probably still be with you."

Still. Yes, she knew all about still. She could recline practically motionless for hours on end, a rare talent. She could do it in the nude, too. A perfect model. A perfect love, for an artist.

No.

Artists didn't need love, and perfection was an ideal to be pursued but never captured.

The work in progress was all that mattered. Anna under the floorboards. Cynthia beneath the canvas. Sharon in the trunk of his Toyota.

And Karen here before him.

His fingers itched, and the reflections of blades gleamed on the work bench.

"I thought you said you could never be happy with an artist," he said. "Because artists are so self-absorbed."

"I never said that, exactly."

Except for three times. Once after making love, when the sheets were sweaty and the breeze so wonderful against the heat of their slick skin, when the city pulsed like a live thing in time to their racing heartbeats, when cars and shouts and bricks and broken glass all paved a trail that led inside each other.

"You said that," he said.

She moved away, turned her back, and pretended to care the least little bit about the Magritte print. "I was younger then."

Karen didn't make mistakes, and if she did, she never admitted them. John didn't know what to make of this new Karen. How did she fit with this new John he was building? Where did she belong in the making?

Art, on a few rare occasions, was born of accident. Or was even accident by design? Karen had entered his life, his studio, his work, right in the midst of his greatest creation. This making of himself.

She walked past the collection of mirror shards he had cemented to the wall. Suddenly there were a dozen Karens, sharp-edged and silvery. All of them with that same fixed smile, one that welcomed itself back to a place it had never truly belonged. John's jagged world.

"What are you working on?" she asked. She'd wondered such things in the beginning, when showing interest in his art was the best way into his head. Then she'd slowly sucked him away, drained his attention until all he could think about was her. She became the centerpiece of his gallery, the showcase, the *magnum opus*. And when at last she'd succeeded in walling him off from his art, when she herself had become the art, along came Henry who called himself Hank.

"Oh, something in soapstone."

The piece was on his bench. She hadn't even noticed. Her eyes were blinded ice.

"Oh, that," she said. "That's pretty neat."

Soapstone had a little give, some flexibility. You could miss your hammer stroke and create an interesting side effect instead of complete and utter rubble. Soapstone could be shaped. Unlike Karen, who was already shaped to near perfection.

The soapstone piece was called 'Madonna and Grapefruit'. Madonna was a long graceful curve, skin splotched by the grain of the stone. Grapefruit was the part he hadn't figured out yet.

He hadn't touched it in four months.

"I'm calling it 'Untitled'," he said. That statement was a lie for the piece called 'Madonna and Grapefruit', but was true for the work in progress for which three women had given their lives.

"Neat. You always were better at sculpting than painting." She looked again at her unfinished portrait on the wall. She added, "But you're a good painter, too."

"So, what's new with you?" As if he had to ask. What was new was that Henry was gone, otherwise she was exactly the same as she'd always been.

"Visiting. My old roommate."

"The sky was two-dimensional," he said.

"What?"

"That day. That day we were talking about a minute ago."

"Don't talk about the past."

"Why not?" he said. "It's all I have."

Her face did a good job of hiding what she was thinking. Marble, or porcelain maybe.

"Where are you staying now?" she asked.

He didn't want to admit that he was sleeping on the couch in the gallery. "I have a walk-up efficiency. Not enough elbow room to get any work done, though. That's why I rent this place."

"So, have you done any shows lately?"

He considered lying, then decided to go for it. "I won second place in a community art show. A hundred bucks and a bag of art supplies."

"Really? Which piece?"

John pointed toward a gnarled wooden monstrosity that sulked in one corner. It had once been a dignified dead oak, but had been debased with hatchet blows and shellac.

"What do you call it?" Karen asked.

"I call it…" John hoped his hesitation played as a dramatic pause while he searched his index of future titles. "I call it 'Moment of Indecision'."

"Heavy."

"I'll say heavy. Weighs over two hundred pounds. I'm surprised it hasn't fallen through the floor."

"And you made a hundred dollars?"

"Well, *make* isn't the right word, if you're calculating profit and loss. I spent forty dollars on materials and put in thirty hours of labor. Comes in at less than half of minimum wage."

He was surprised how fast he was talking now. And it was all due to Karen walking toward the rumpled canvas in the corner, leaning over it, examining the lumps and folds and probably wondering what great treasure lay underneath.

The artist formerly known as Cynthia.

"Say, Karen, how's your old roommate?" The same roommate who wouldn't leave the room so they could make love in Karen's tiny bed. The roommate who thought John was stuck up. The roommate who was so desperately and hideously blonde that John wished for a moment she could become part of the work in progress.

The distraction worked, because Karen turned from the canvas and stroked a nest of wires that was trying to become a postmodern statement.

"She's the same as ever," Karen said.

"Aren't we all?" John looked at the handles of the steak knives. They almost formed the outline of a letter of the alphabet.

"I don't know why I'm here. I really shouldn't be here."

"Don't say that. It's really good to see you."

John pictured her as a metal dolphin, leaping from the water, drops falling like golden rust against the sunset. Frozen in a moment of decision. A single framed image that he could never paint.

He looked at the oil of Karen. The endless work in progress. Maybe if he ran a streak of silver along that left breast, the angle of the moonlight would trick the viewer.

If Karen wasn't here, such a moment of inspiration would have brought a mad rush for brushes and paints. Now, he felt foolish.

Because Karen was here after all. This was life, not art. This was life, not art. This was life, not art.

He clenched one fist behind his back.

Ah.

Untitled.

Sharon in the trunk of his Toyota.

"The sky was two-dimensional," John said.

"What?"

"That day."

"John." She picked up his fluter, a wedged piece of metal. Nobody touched his fluter.

"What?"

She nodded toward The Painting, the one that showed most of her nude body. "Did you like painting me just because you could get me naked that way?"

A question that had two possible answers. Yes or no.

The artist always chose the third possible answer.

"Both," he said. "How's Henry?"

"Hank. At least that's what his boyfriend calls him." Karen wiggled her hands into the pockets of her blue jeans. Tightening the fabric.

John's fingers itched.

"So, how's the job?" he asked.

As if he had to ask. Accounting. The same as always.

"The same as always," she said. "I got another raise last year."

The ladder and how to climb it. Karen knew the book by heart, learned by rote at the feet of Henry who called himself Hank. Or was it Hank who changed his name to Henry?

Such confusion.

So many sharp edges and reflections.

"Why are you here?" John asked.

"I already told you."

"No. I mean, really."

She picked up a piece of colored glass, a remnant from a miniature church John had built and then smashed. She held the glass to her eye and looked through. Blue behind blue.

"I got to wondering about you," she said. "How you were getting along and all that. And I wanted to see how famous artists lived."

Famous artists didn't live. All the most famous artists were long dead, and the ones who swayed the critics during their own lifetimes made John suspicious.

"I'm the most famous artist nobody's ever heard of," he said.

She rubbed her thumb along the edge of the glass. "That's one thing I don't miss about you. Your insecurity."

"Artists have to go to dangerous places. You can't get too comfortable if you want to make a statement."

Karen put the piece of blue glass on the desk beside his mallet. She went to the portrait again. She pointed to the curve of her painted hip. "Maybe if you put a little more red here."

"Maybe."

She turned. "This is really sad, John. You promised you were going to throw yourself into your work and make me regret ever breaking up with you."

He hated her for knowing him so well. Knowing him, but not understanding. That was something he'd never been able to forgive her for.

But then, she wasn't perfect. She was a work in progress, too.

"You can't even finish one lousy painting," she said.

"I've been working on my crow collection."

"Crow collection? What the hell is that?"

"Shiny stuff. Spiritual stuff."

"I thought you were going to make that series of twelve that was going to be your ticket to the top."

He looked out the window. The room smelled of kerosene and decay.

She waved her hands at the mess on the workbench. "You gave up me for this."

No. She left him for Hank or Henry. John never made the choice. She wanted him to give up art. That was never an option.

"I guess I'd better get going," she said.

He thought about grabbing her, hugging her, whispering to her the way he had in the old days. He wanted her naked, posing. Then, perhaps, he could finish the portrait.

"It was really good to see you," he said.

"Yeah." Her face was pale, a mixture of peach and titanium white.

She paused by the studio door and took a last look at The Painting. "Frozen in time," she said.

"No, it's not frozen at all. It's a work in progress."

"See you around."

Not likely, since she lived two thousand miles away. The door closed with a soft squeak, a sigh of surrender.

John looked at the portrait again.

Karen here before him.

Not the one who walked and breathed, the one he could never shape. *This* was the Karen he could possess. The real Karen. The Painting.

He possessed them all. Anna under the floorboards. Cynthia beneath the canvas. Sharon in the trunk of his Toyota.

John hurried to the bench and grabbed up his tools.

The Muse had spoken. He realized he'd never wanted to build himself, or dream himself alive. Art wasn't about sacrificing for the good of the artist. Art was about sacrificing for others.

For Karen.

She was the real work in progress, the one that could be improved. The canvas awaited his touch.

John uncovered Cynthia and went to work. By midnight, The Painting was finished.

It was perfection.

THE FROZEN LAKE

JOHN SHIRLEY

"We only have one computer," Judith said. "We couldn't have two lines."

"This is...2019 Coolidge? Roy Breedlaw lives here?" The man from the internet cable company, looking closer at his clipboard, was a chunky Hispanic guy with a round, pleasant face and a mustache that made her think of her dad – who'd been dead forty years. His soft voice made her think of dad too, maybe because it was March. Dad had died in the frozen lake, back in Minnesota, one unseasonably cold March.

"Yes, that's the right address, Roy's my husband – but we don't have a cable line for the attic."

"Says here you do. Anyway I can see the cable there. You see it, there, ma'am?"

She covered her eyes against the drizzle and squinted up at the eaves over the driveway. She didn't have her glasses on. She tended to wear them only when she was driving or watching television. "Oh gosh... You sure that's what that is? Maybe it's the other line, that just passes through there."

"No ma'am, that one's over there, you see?"

"Oh." So Roy had installed an extra line without telling her. This man must think she was clueless. It made her stomach clutch up to think about it. "And you need to go up into the attic?"

"Yes ma'am. The box's got some kind of short in it. Probably water leaking in. Your husband asked to meet me here, on Monday, but you know how hard it can be for us with the timing. We missed him, so I came back today."

"Yes, yes I..." Monday, she thought, when she wouldn't be home. She was working three days a week now at Ronald Reagan Elementary. Mrs Ramirez had physical therapy three days a week for the rest of the term. Roy knew she was gone on Mondays. He didn't want her to know about the cable in the attic. He didn't like people up there. "I'll get you a ladder, it's the only way to get up there. You have to climb up from the outside."

"From outside of the garage? That's unusual."

"I... He took the original indoor ladder out, to keep the kids out. He was afraid they'd get into trouble there." As she said it, she was conscious of how peculiar it sounded. She decided not to tell him about how Roy had rebuilt the attic just to house his model shop. Most men would have simply done the work on a bench in their garage – which was meticulous, uncluttered, with plenty of room to work.

"Not a problem, ma'am, I have a ladder, but thank you."

"Oh wait – it's locked. I do have a key..." Should she give it to him? Roy said to unlock it only if there was smoke coming out, a fire of some kind. Otherwise no one was to go in. But there was a short, which could cause a fire. That's what she would tell Roy, anyway, when he asked why she'd given the man the key.

She took the keyring from the pocket of her housedress, twisted the padlock key off, and gave it to him. He took an extending ladder from his truck, climbed it to the little door over the deck, in back, that led into the attic room over the garage.

Judith waited on the front porch, watching the cat melting in and out of the geraniums, waiting, imagining what it would be like to be married to this internet cable man. He probably liked to barbecue with the family, take little camping trips. It'd be nice.

She kind of wished the weather would just get on with it and rain. But it didn't rain that much, after February, this side of San Francisco Bay. She started to pull weeds from the garden, almost haphazardly, wondering why it bothered her so much to give someone permission to go in Roy's attic. It was ludicrous, really.

The cable man was smiling when he came back out front, chuckling about all the models that Roy kept up there. "Someone sure can craft models. Airplanes and every sort of thing." He handed her back the key.

"Yep, my husband doesn't care, just as long as it's a good model."

She'd actually only seen a few of them. Sometimes he brought one down when he was finished, to show, for a few seconds. No one was allowed to touch it, though.

He tilted his ladder and collapsed it down so he could carry it to the truck. "I guess the kids have a good time with that too," he said, easily taking the ladder under his arm.

Almost immediately she said, "Oh sure, they have a good time with that."

She didn't want to tell this stranger that Roy wouldn't let the kids up there, didn't ever put models together with them.

Brandon would have liked the models, but Roy wouldn't let him near them. Cherie had never seemed interested in doing things with Roy. It was enough if her stepdad came to her high school's talent show, and only because she wanted two parents there. Of course, she'd have preferred Barry. But Judith had divorced Barry, after his affair, and he'd moved to Los Angeles to be with the woman he'd been sleeping with. They didn't see him much. Roy didn't like him coming around.

Judith waved as the man went to his van. She watched him drive away and then she went to get the ladder Roy used.

"Mrs Breedlaw?"

"Hm?"

"Paper or plastic."

"Oh – paper... Um, no – plastic. Plastic's fine." Judith had noticed a flicker of irritation on the bagger's face when she said paper, because they already had the plastic bag laid out in a little metal frame, and it was easier for them. So she went with plastic, though she preferred paper bags. Maybe I should just up and say 'paper' and the heck with him, she thought. Joe Gorris, at the school, said she wasn't assertive enough with her students. She 'let them run roughshod' over her in class. She knew she tended to be that way.

She looked to see if Brandon was still staring at the little shiny toys in the gumball machine, things he'd have swallowed and choked on just a few years ago when he was going through his swallowing phase. He was there, his lips moving silently. A small black girl in corn-rows and a Sponge Bob T-shirt came to stand near him, admiring the HomiePals dolls in the machine: wizened little hip-hop figures on shiny keychains. The girl turned to stare at Brandon, puzzled. He was a tall thirteen, too old to be enchanted by the machine. It was one of his autistic things – he didn't do it so much as he used to, though.

"Brandon, let's go!" she called, pushing the cart up near him, on the way to the door.

He didn't acknowledge her directly, of course, but he turned to go toward the door with her, and they walked side by side without speaking. He didn't ask for shiny things from gumball machines any more. The shiny things he looked at now were on MTV: Christina Aguilera especially. It kind of broke Judith's heart to see it. Even if Brandon had a girl, not just a pretty girl like that but any girl, he'd probably be afraid to let her touch him.

Brandon was getting better, she reminded herself. He was more in control of himself. He didn't do that spinning around anymore; he answered questions, most of the time. He was making some progress. The therapist she'd gone to for herself, before Roy had decided it was too expensive, had said she should look at the positive things going on in her life, to break up that depression spiral. She didn't get depressed much anyway, now, with the Prozac. It was a low dose, but it worked well enough.

She and Brandon went out to the Explorer. It was still misting outside. About halfway through loading the groceries, Brandon started to help her.

The wind was rising, she noticed. She hadn't gotten the palm trees clipped and they'd be throwing their old branches at the house again. *Fronds*, they're called, she reminded herself. But they were five and six feet long, with a piece of wood on the end, when they dropped off, more like branches to her.

She hoped Roy wasn't home when she got there, though she wasn't sure why she hoped for it.

Judith kept a damp cloth in the freezer for her hot flushes, and she was pressing that to her head when Roy came in the front door. She could tell by the abruptness of the sound that it was him, and not Cherie. She put the washcloth back. When Roy saw her treating her menopause symptoms in any way, he acted as if she were trying to prod him into some outburst of sympathy. "I don't want to hear about it," he'd say. "If you need to go to a doctor, go, but all women dry up that way..." That last remark had been a stunning new level of insensitivity, even for Roy.

Now he came into the kitchen, frowning. "Has someone been up in the attic?"

How had he known, already? she wondered, drifting out to the living room. It was a bigger room – she didn't like being with him in so small a room as the kitchen. She was glad of the menopause, in a way, because before the change she'd felt more like being in bed with a man; someone, but not with Roy, and now she didn't much feel like sex with anyone. Roy hadn't asked for a long time and it was just as well. She didn't know if she could stand another of those sessions where he rubbed himself on her till he got excited, squeezing his eyes tight shut so she could tell he was picturing something else, and then making those oil-derrick pumpings into her. He'd made her feel like there was something wrong with her, when she'd tried to talk about their sex life. She had shrugged and accepted him that way – she hadn't married him for sex, anyway. And she couldn't go through another divorce.

"The cable man said there might be a short there or something, so I gave him the key," she said, sounding as reasonable as she could. "You were going to have him up there anyway, on Monday."

She could tell by the way her husband was moving around the room, almost running as he went from object to object, flattening wrinkles on doilies, wiping dust from the tops of picture frames, that he was going to start shouting. She noticed that he'd changed the part in his hair again, to the other side. Every so often he shifted the part, and when he parted his stiff brown hair on the right side of his head it looked all wrong, somehow. His eyebrows were too light for his hair and it was always difficult to see what color his eyes were, because of his heavy lids; you had to really look close to see they were a sort of greenish brown. When they met he'd looked slightly odd but the oddity had grown over the years, as if his face were put together from parts of the faces of three men. He'd grown into his penchant for khaki pants and those golf shirts with the little alligators over the breast, too. He even wore that outfit to church – he never missed church. He had been in the choir for a long time. He had a nice singing voice, a pure alto. It seemed more than fifteen years since they'd met in the choir. He'd come over to practice parts, and she'd play piano, and they'd sing. They started doing show tunes, and then he'd asked her out. He'd had a sense of humor, sometimes, in those days. He'd sold the piano, four years ago, to help pay for suing a man who'd sideswiped his car. He'd stopped singing in the choir about the same time.

"You were told: *only if there's a fire,*" he was saying, adjusting the shade on a lamp.

"I was afraid there could be a fire, because he said there might be a short." Change the subject, she thought. "We got calls from some attorney's office asking when we're going to make a payment on his legal bill? I didn't know you'd sued anybody else till she said – "

"Have those kids been moving things around in here?" he asked suddenly, the volume of his voice elevating two notches. His eyes darted to the ceiling, in the direction of the garage. "That chair wasn't so close to the wall." He moved it six inches toward the center of the room.

He meant Brandon mostly. Cherie mostly managed to not be home when Roy was there. "No. Roy, the kids have hardly been here. Now please – how are we going to pay for this lawsuit? We can't pay for it by winning, they told me you already lost it – "

"The man was letting his bushes grow over our fence, and it was dropping seeds all over our land, and sending up shoots, and the roots from them damaged our pipes!"

"It just doesn't seem like...like a priority thing, Roy – "

"Are you telling me what's important in my life?" he demanded, turning to her, commencing the brittle monotone shouting that she'd known was coming.

When her first husband, Barry, had shouted at her, he looked right at her and it'd felt kind of good, because she'd known he was just letting off steam and afterward they'd make up and even make love. When they were signing the divorce papers, he'd said he was sorry he'd ever yelled at her. Funny time to say it.

Roy's yelling was so much worse. He shouted at her but never looked at her as he did it.

"I have to ask, Roy, because we don't want to have to move again."

"I'm getting a settlement, is that what you want to hear? Well I am, from the county, and you're driving my blood pressure up, you're trying to kill me!"

She instinctively reached to pat his arm because the high blood pressure remark made her want to help him calm down, but he'd come to dislike being touched – maybe he'd always disliked it – and he pulled away, shouted at her to keep the kids away from his things.

"You didn't tell me we had another computer in the house. A second line."

"What is it, because your last husband had an affair, you're putting that on me? Did he meet her on the internet? That's not me. I am not him. Okay? I am researching things, the law, things like that. That's what I need it for. I want to work undisturbed. I told you, you just weren't listening. I have to research this, it's complicated as all Hell..."

He lectured her about the court case for a while, and how he wasn't going to let people damage his property. Judith was relieved when he finally went up to his attic.

He'd never told her about the extra internet line. She was sure of that.

She went to the family room, where Brandon was playing videogames. She leaned against the doorframe and watched him. It was a game with a Chinese name she couldn't remember, where you had to move a doll-like man in a gaudy warrior's outfit around, so that he fought giant wizards and dragons. But sometimes the hero had to interact with friendly figures, and Brandon was making him approach a voluptuous big-eyed girl, wearing a sort of scaly looking bikini and boots. He made his hero do a kind of dance-step near her, so that she jumped back. Then his character leapt backwards, and that made her jump toward him. It didn't seem to be anything that advanced the game, but he kept at it, making the characters dance together as best he could.

Judith went to him, bent, and kissed him on top of the head. He took one hand off the controller, reached out, and patted the toe of her shoe, then went back to playing.

She smiled, feeling a little better, and went up to the sewing room she used as an office, to prep for class. It felt good to be teaching. If she could find a way to pay for the night school she could get a teacher's certificate, work with special ed kids full time. Roy didn't want to pay for the classes though. Money going to lawsuits couldn't be spared for classes. Maybe she could get a second job.

Late afternoon, coming home from work, she looked at her watch and decided Roy wouldn't be there for at least an hour. She had time to go into the attic.

She actually went *into* the attic room, this visit. After the cable man had left she'd gone up to lock the door and, really, to have a look inside. She just looked around at the models, and confirmed for herself he had a computer in there she didn't know about. A Dell laptop, connected to an HP printer.

On the right side of the garage attic Roy had set up a big, pretty thick piece of fiberboard over two sawhorses. It was bright with coronas of spray paint, but all Roy's modeling tools were neatly lined on it. To the left of the workbench, under the nailed-shut half-moon window with the frosted glass, a cable ran to a laptop computer on a small workstation desk that looked like it had come from Staples. She'd never seen the desk before.

Bent over, under the roof, she slipped down a narrow opening between the models and sat on the old piano stool he used for a seat in front of the laptop table. You had to sit or stoop, in here.

This time, looking around, she realized she just didn't want to be around Roy any more than she had to, not because of the things she knew he was prone to do but because he was a stranger, really, and she was afraid of feeling she was alone in the house with a stranger. Strangers might do things you couldn't anticipate.

People talked about finding out that they didn't know the people they were married to. But she didn't think they were experiencing it as completely as she was. She'd been married to him for ten years and she'd created a sort of model of him, her own glued-together model, in her mind. She used that model as her Roy. But that wasn't him.

Looking at the models, now – by Revelle and Astra and PlasCo – she felt like she was in some kind of Indian medicine man's cave. She didn't know why, but it felt that way, like something she'd seen on the Discovery channel. Maybe it was partly the way the wind groaned over the roof. So much louder than you'd hear it downstairs. It sounded angry.

The models were hanging from the inverted-V ceiling on fishing line, some lines longer than others so the models were all at about the same level. Even the ones that weren't models of flying things, like the PT boat from World War II, hung dangling from the ceiling. Lots of the models were from World War II, but some were from the Vietnam War, like the MiG and a helicopter. The Monitor and the Merrimac were from the Civil War. There were some cars, too, hanging from the ceiling. Who would hang cars from the ceiling? But plastic models of cars rotated slowly in the dusty air: a GTO and a Mustang and some kind of Mercury she wasn't sure of.

All of the models were perfectly made, without too much glue, without fingerprints, with smooth, expert use of modeling spraypaint, no paint where it shouldn't be. He trimmed the parts with emery boards and one-sided razorblades when they needed help fitting together. And all the parts fitted together exactly.

What especially made her think she knew Roy even less than she'd thought had to do with the miniature plastic people on the models. Roy had gotten them at Kroner's Hobbies, probably, and he'd gotten a tiny little paintbrush, with just two hairs on it – she could see it on his work desk – and he had painted a crooked line across each figure's neck. Every single one of the tiny figures, women in the cars and men in the planes and on the boats, was painted to show a purple and red line across their tiny little throats. The line was the color of a bruise.

She reached up and idly tapped one of the planes, a B-52, or something close to it. It spun around, with its tiny little man in the roof gunner's bubble, staring out at the whirling attic, showing the mark on his throat when he turned her way, spinning to look at the other models, showing the mark again. She reached out to stop the spinning and there came a loud crunching bang from the ceiling and she recoiled, her hand knocking into the model so it rocked violently into the back of the GTO. The little plastic trunk of the toy GTO popped off.

She sat with her fists balled white in her lap, staring at the broken model, listening. But she knew what the bang was, it was the frond from a palm tree shedding in the high wind. There were serrated edges like little shark teeth on each frond and they came down hard on the roof like a drumstick on a tom-tom, the whole house vibrating when they struck. She was glad Brandon was at the training center, the thumps always scared him.

She shook her head, feeling sheepish. The branch hitting the roof had scared her. It had made her feel like Roy was shouting at her for being in his sanctum; for touching his things.

She looked at her watch, as she waited for her pulse to slow. It was four o'clock. Roy wouldn't be home, likely, for another hour and fifteen minutes. Because of his blood pressure, Roy was working part time. His job for the county, assessing road damage and repair, was kind of dicey right now, since he was also suing the county, claiming they'd given him a disability – she didn't really understand the claim. But there was no talking to him about his lawsuits.

Letting out a long breath, Judith got up, careful not to bump her head. She found the trunk lid of the model GTO on the floor. It looked like it would fit neatly back on the car. But when she went to put it on, she saw a papery something rolled up in the trunk of the model GTO. She hesitated, then plucked it out, using the tips of her fingernails to get at it. She unrolled the paper. It was a small cutting from a digital-photo printout. Someone had clipped it from a bigger picture.

It was a photograph of a girl in the trunk of a car. She had a ball-gag in her mouth and her arms and feet were tied with rope. That was Roy's car. You could see the outline of the Taurus's rear fender, and you could just make out the top of the bumper sticker that said: WWJD? *What Would Jesus Do?*

"I told her no way was I going to get into the play but she said, 'Oh just audition' and I did and they gave me the part of Betty Rizzo and it's like the second best part in *Grease* – Mom are you listening?"

"What? Yes! Oh my God that's so great, you got…Betty Rizzo!"

Cherie laughed, not something she often did spontaneously, and flipped through the script in her lap. She was a bottle blonde, she had that straight hair with just the suggestion of a curl at the bottom that celebrities had been affecting last year, but to Judith it looked like a haystack. She had some acne, and Barry's small nose, but she wasn't an unattractive girl, by any means, and she had a decent singing voice. Her blue eyes – Barry's eyes – shone with a kind of derisive joy now. "You don't even know who Betty Rizzo is! You don't even know that musical!"

"It's true," Judith said, "I've never seen it, but I'm going to learn all about it – I have to help you memorize your lines!"

She had found a picture in each of four other models, the ones she could open without leaving an obvious trace. Four different young women, about Cherie's age. All were dead now.

"Mrs Duwitt said it's the biggest play the senior class has done in years, and – *and!* – Nathan's in it!"

Roy had killed all those girls, and some others. She recognized one of the girls from her picture in the paper, two years ago. Missing, foul play suspected.

"*Nathan?* Oh my gosh! Do you think you guys'll get back together?"

"I think so. I think he wanted an excuse to. I'm not mad at him anymore. I don't think he was really into Miranda."

It all came together now. A hundred little suspicions, converged like loose bricks becoming a house. She had thought for a long time Roy was hiding things, more than just lawsuits. She'd thought it was an affair. But then she'd wondered about worse things. Could he be stalking someone? Taking pictures in some girls' locker room? Something. But this... She remembered when he'd videotaped the news shows, for a long time, months. He'd said it was so he could talk to Cherie about current events, but they never talked about them. At about that time, more than half the news shows contained something about the SP Killer. *SP* for *Smile Pretty*, because he would take photos of the girls, tied up and terrified and about to die, and he'd sent the first of them to the police, with the caption SMILE PRETTY! printed on it. He videotaped more than just the shows that mentioned the SP Killer. He'd been careful to do that. But he'd gotten all the SP stories, she realized now.

There were some closed boxes in the attic along one wall. He must keep the videotapes in there. What else was on them?

"Are you okay, Mom? You're not doing those afternoon cocktails again."

"What? No, you know I gave up drinking. I... Why?"

"You're so, like, distracted."

"I'm just so amazed by this great development for you."

Brandon came into the room, not looking at his sister, but he'd been listening and he said, as if to the air, "Great development. Cool Cherie."

Cherie smiled. "Thanks Brandon."

The papers speculated that the SP Killer met the girls on the internet. All the girls had been doing internet dating, or hanging about in chat-rooms. But so far no one had traced the murderer that way. They'd tried everything to catch him. He was careful. He tortured them to death. But he was careful.

It wasn't careful, though, to keep the pictures. But then, all these people – it was hard to even think the words *serial killer* – almost all of them kept trophies. She'd seen a show about it on CourtTV. Roy had watched with her. He'd watched silently, closely. Annoyed when she ventured a comment.

"Tell Dad," Brandon said, looking into the air.

Cherie and her mother looked at Brandon. Brandon was trying to say that Dad would be proud of Cherie, Judith supposed.

Cherie snorted. She knew better. Judith said, "I sure will tell him. We'll both be there on opening night."

She should go to the police right now. He was out tonight. He was supposed to be bowling. He did take a bowling bag with him. She'd never met the guys he bowled with. They'd never gotten a phone message from them on the answering machine.

He was out there right now, with that bag.

"And it's just so cool," Cherie went on, crossing the gap in her happiness, the 'tell Dad' lacuna. "I've got two songs with Nathan, we have to rehearse together a *lot –* "

Roy had tried to talk to Judith, once, about two years ago. Maybe he had been trying to tell her about his compulsions. *Do you ever feel, Judith, like you're already dead in your coffin and you're just remembering your life? You're laying in your coffin rotting and your ghost is stuck in there and whatever seems like it's happening to you now is just that dead person remembering this day. So you have to find some way to get out of the coffin, you might have to be real destructive to get out...*

No, she'd said. *I can't really imagine that.* She hadn't encouraged him to go on. She'd been terrified by this sudden confidence, the unmitigated blackness of this disclosure.

She should have drawn him out, she saw now. This was her fault.

"And Nathan loves to do choreography – are you listening, Mom?"

"Yes! Yes I am. So you'll be dancing with Nathan as part of the show?"

He would tie them up and slowly strangle them, very slowly, the coroner had said. Making those red and brown marks on their necks, like the ones he'd painted on the miniature plastic people. *Very slowly.*

She had slept beside him for years.

"Mom? You are totally spacing on me. I'm gonna go call Lina anyway, she doesn't know, she's going to freak!"

She was sure there was a picture in every one of the plastic models, even the ones she hadn't opened up.

He was out right now with his bag.

She should call the police. She could call them right now.

Roy didn't say much when Judith told him she had decided she was going to sleep in her sewing room, "for awhile." She would never be able to sleep beside him again.

He accepted her explanation about the hot flushes making her thrash around. Not wanting to disturb him. "Whatever, whatever," he said, taking a new Revelle model, some kind of dragster, out of a paper bag. "I'm going to work on this model." He folded the paper bag, put it carefully in the little kitchen closet he kept folded paper bags in, then carried the model out back, and set up his ladder.

She could hear him crossing the roof over the deck, and going into his attic room. He hadn't taken the bowling bag with him. He had stashed it somewhere else. He must have the digital camera in his coat. They were small devices.

She went to her sewing room, and pulled out the bed in the compact sofa. The wind was still pushing at the house, outside. The walls creaked with it.

Judith locked the door, and lay on the sofa bed, stretched out, with just the small lamp beside her sewing machine turned on. She lay on her back, looking at the ceiling, wanting a drink so badly. She didn't care about getting started drinking again, but she needed to think with clarity now. She couldn't afford to be drunk.

Had he killed someone tonight? Was he printing the murdered girl's picture now?

Judith remembered watching her father die, on the frozen lake, in Minnesota. It had been dusk, in early March. She'd been ten years old. Her father had been out on the lake, trying to fish through a hole in the ice with one of his friends. They'd had too much beer and they'd started pushing each other, laughing and floundering around, and the ice had broken. Only her daddy had fallen through.

Emergency rescue had been sent for and people tried different things to get him out. Her mother had kept her back from the lake but she'd climbed a tree to see what was happening to her daddy and from up above she could see the blurry outline of a man thrashing around under the ice, drifting too far away from the hole he'd fallen through. People were yelling at him, "Don't use up your strength trying to crack the ice, Jim! Don't do that, just tread water! Tread water and wait, you'll make it, we'll get you out in a minute, we're gonna cut through! Just hold on – *don't do that, Jim!*"

But Dad panicked and couldn't keep himself from trying to break through the ice. He kept trying to hammer at it but his efforts were carrying him farther and farther from the hole and he was getting more and more exhausted and then he sank down, out of sight, and they didn't get his body out for a couple of days...

Judith could hear her daughter in her bedroom, muffled through the wall so she couldn't make out what she was saying. She was on her cellphone to one of her friends, telling them about being in the show;

telling them every detail. The happiness was apparent in her voice, even if the words weren't coming through to Judith.

Most of the time, Cherie was morose. Now she was going to be happy, at least for a while. She had a part in a musical at school, and the guy she wanted to get back together with was in the play, too. She might never be happier in life.

If Judith turned her husband in, that would end. Everything good in Cherie's life would end, maybe forever.

Brandon was getting better. Measurably, anyhow. He had a really good special ed teacher who spoke warmly of him.

If she'd tolerated Barry's affair, it probably would've run its course, and they'd still be together.

But this wasn't like finding out about an affair. This was finding out your husband was a monster. She had to stop him. She had to turn him in.

Of course, with her husband in the papers and on the TV news, she would probably have to move away. Living here, with everyone knowing her husband was the SP Killer – unbearable. They'd have to start someplace else. If they were allowed to, by the police. They'd want her around to testify.

They'd have to sell the house to pay for lawyers. Roy would never accept a public defender. She paid for Brandon's teachers, now. The public schools had done so little for him. Brandon would lose that.

The police might not arrest Roy instantly. He might take revenge on her. He might kill her and Cherie and Brandon. Especially Cherie. She wasn't his daughter. He'd probably thought about killing her. But if he'd killed her, the police would look at him too closely. If she looked like she was going to turn him in, he'd have nothing to lose. He might kill them all.

And the people. *"She married the SP Killer. She had to have known. Some way you'd have to know. How could you not know? Come on. She knew. She knew!"*

She loved being a substitute teacher. That would end. The principal would be apologetic, but he'd let her go. *"The parents get freaked out, Judith. You understand."*

She'd never be hired to teach again.

She ought to go to the police. Already someone more might've died because she'd delayed. If she knew and didn't tell, she was in complicity, whether the police found out about her knowing, or not. It was moral complicity. She was helping him kill those girls. There was a greater good. She had to go to the police.

A *thump!* from the roof. The palm tree had thrown another clublike frond at her.

If she turned Roy in, Cherie would know that her stepdad was the SP Killer and she'd always have to live with that and it would ruin Cherie's life. There was no telling what effect it could have on Brandon. How could it be good?

What else could she do? She imagined herself killing Roy – putting a pillow over his mouth as he slept. Putting all her weight on his face.

She wouldn't mind that, not at all. If she thought it would work. But she wouldn't be any good at killing him. He'd wake up and he'd grab her and he'd realize she knew and he'd kill her and then maybe Cherie and Brandon.

So she had to go to the police.

Cherie's voice was still coming through the wall from her bedroom. It was wordless, and happy. Like a song hummed instead of sung, by someone happy to be alive.

Judith's father had thrashed and struggled and tried to break out of the ice, and the cold water had borne him down and they'd found him face down, floating in a layer of muck near the bottom.

He should have just gone on treading water till they'd gotten him out.

She could do that. She could tread water. She could tread water until some chance came to get out of the frozen lake. Cherie could be happy until then; Brandon could go on as he was, until then. Maybe Roy would stop killing. He might. Sometimes they did. She'd read that. They stopped eventually.

She wasn't murdering those girls. Roy was doing it. He was the one doing it. And after all most of these girls were either prostitutes or slutty girls he'd picked up on the internet. They shouldn't be meeting men on the internet.

If a few more had to die, that had to be all right. She had to let it happen. She had to keep treading water. The lake was cold, and dark.

It was him. Not her. It wasn't her doing. She could sleep in the sewing room.

Shelley Costa's 'Black Heart and Cabin Girl' was nominated for the 2004 Edgar Award by Mystery Writers of America. Her short stories have appeared in *Crimewave*, *The Georgia Review* and *The World's Finest Mystery & Crime Stories*. She's on the faculty of the Cleveland Institute of Art, where she teaches creative writing.

Mick Scully currently lives and works in Birmingham. Much of his writing centres around the Little Moscow, a notorious bar frequented by the city's criminal fraternity. A collection of his stories, *Tales from the Little Moscow*, is being published by Tindal Street Press in May 2007.

Gary W. Shockley and his wife Lori Ann White have just returned from a trip to South America. Among the highlights of the trip: a volcano in Ecuador spewing ash all the while they were in a small resort on its slope; climbing as high as they could, meeting the 'volcano watcher' who hangs out in an insane tree house and claims he can give a 20-minute warning of an eruption; the thing in the toilet, big as a hand, piecemeal illuminated by flashlight in a spooky game of hide-and-seek that went on for minutes, in the middle of a night in the Peruvian rainforest; a tarantula sleeping around the base of a kerosine lamp; putting his hand in the mouth of a tapir; photographing a wild owl monkey in the night as it emerged from a hollow (from two metres away) in the rainforest canopy. Gary and Lori (a writer herself) hope to tap these experiences for future stories.

Ron Savage has been publishing his stories since the age of eighteen. They have appeared in journals and magazines throughout the world. His more recent publications include the *Taj Mahal Review* in India, the *Lichen Review* in Canada, and the *Southern Humanities Review*. Ron has a BA and MA in psychology and a doctorate in counselling from The College of William and Mary. He has worked as an actor, a broadcaster, a newspaper editor, and for twenty-something years as Psychologist Senior at Eastern State Hospital in Williamsburg. He has recently retired from everything but his writing and his lovely wife Jan.

Originally an engineer from Houston, Texas, **Susan Overcash Walker** is currently pursuing a second life as a writer and a Master of Fine Arts degree in Creative Writing from the University of North Carolina-Greensboro. She now lives in Clayton, North Carolina, with her husband and two dogs.

In the last three years, **Scott William Carter** has sold over two dozen stories to such places as *Analog*, *Asimov's*, *Ellery Queen's*, *Realms of Fantasy* and *Weird Tales*, as well as to anthologies by Pocket Books and DAW. He lives in Oregon with his patient wife and two young children. Find out more about his work at www.scottwilliamcarter.com

Daniel Bennett was born in 1974. He studied at the University of East Anglia and the University of Colorado and now lives in South London with his wife and daughter. He has stories forthcoming in *Black Static* and his first novel, *All the Dogs*, will be published in 2007 by Tindal Street Press.

Ian R. Faulkner was born in the West Midlands in 1966 and he has yet to escape, although he hopes one day they will let him out on day release, as writing with crayons is really very difficult. His first published story, 'Lost in Darkness' (co-written with Simon Avery), appeared in *Crimewave 8: Cold Harbours* and has since been reprinted in Maxim Jakubowski's anthology *The Best British Mysteries IV*. His hobbies include obsessively collecting books, comics, CDs and films on DVD, and, if he's not watched closely, anything else he can lay his hands on.

Robert Weston's fiction has appeared in literary magazines on both sides of the Atlantic. His work has been nominated for the Journey Prize and the Fountain Award for Speculative Literature. A forthcoming story will soon appear in *Postscripts*. Currently, he lives in Vancouver, where he has just completed an epic novel for children.

Kevin Prufer is the author of four books of poetry, the newest of which are *Fallen from a Chariot* (Carnegie Mellon University Press, 2005) and *National Anthem* (Four Way Books, forthcoming). With Wayne Miller, he's editor of both *The New European Poetry* (Graywolf Press, forthcoming) and *Pleiades: A Journal of New Writing*. His mystery stories have appeared recently in *Alfred Hitchcock's Mystery Magazine*. He lives in rural Missouri, USA. He can be found online at www.kevinprufer.com

Scott Nicholson is the author of six novels, including *The Farm* and *The Home*. His vampire novel *They Hunger* will be released in April 2007. He lives in the Blue Ridge Mountains of North Carolina, where he tends an organic garden, eats sushi, and dreams of raising goats. His spirit lives at www.hauntedcomputer.com

John Shirley is the author of numerous books and many, many short stories. His novels include *Crawlers*, *Demons*, *In Darkness Waiting* and seminal cyberpunk works *City Come A-Walkin'* and the *A Song Called Youth* trilogy. His collections include the award-winning *Black Butterflies* and *Really Really Really Really Weird Stories*. He also writes for screen (*The Crow*) and television.

Crimewave 9: Transgressions was printed properly by the craftsmen of Cambridge University Press. Original high quality fiction will return in **Crimewave 10**. Secure your copy now by subscribing. Each issue is much bigger than it ought to be, making a four-issue subscription (£22 UK • £26 EUROPE • £30 ROW) even greater value. You can subscribe by post with a cheque/PO payable to TTA Press, 5 Martins Lane, Witcham, Ely, Cambs CB6 2LB, UK; securely online at www.ttapress.com/onlinestore1.html; or by PayPal to TTA Press. Remember: make no mistake, it's still a jaguar.